LATTES AND LIES

CHRISTINE ZANE THOMAS
WILLIAM TYLER DAVIS

Edited by
ELLEN CAMPBELL

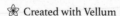

1

Waiting there on her porch was the hardest part. I fidgeted with my collar, shifted my weight from the left to the right foot, then moved the bouquet of flowers from one hand to the other. It was a fall mix—daisies, Gerbera daisies, and roses. It's the thought that counts. Plus, I knew Gerbera daisies were her favorite.

I rapped again, twice this time. The door, like the shutters of the cottage, was red.

Still, there was no answer.

My legs were aching from all this standing. It had been a long day—a long several days of work at Kapow Koffee, my comic book and coffee shop—and the week wasn't over yet. Being the owner came with duties like unpacking boxes of new comics late into most Tuesday nights, and at least twice this week I'd worked a double shift when one of my four employees, Sarah, was out with a cold. Only two more days, Friday and Saturday, before I got the much needed day off on Sunday.

Sweat beaded on my brow. It was a warm October evening.

Florida did its best to stave off the fall season as long as possible. This was what passed as fall in northern Florida—muggy humidity, gnats and mosquitoes swarming around my face, and sweat. My armpits, which'd already stained this particular white undershirt, were slippery with it. I only hoped it didn't seep through to my button-down shirt.

I was dressed nice this evening. The shirt, khaki pants, deck shoes in place of flip-flops. I was ready to go. But it seemed my date wasn't.

A whiff of the flowers breezed into my nostrils. The sweet smell was almost too much to take. They'd been left in the shop only the day before. After finding them on the seat of a booth while cleaning up for the night, I spent all morning asking each patron if the flowers belonged to them. They hadn't. And it seemed a shame to let them go to waste.

How long has she been? How long have I been standing here? I wondered. *This has gone on long enough.*

I went to open the door—she usually left it unlocked. But when I did, my date was about one foot from it. She jumped back a few feet and the casserole dish she was carrying clattered to the wood floor.

"Kirby Jackson!" Memaw wailed. "You almost scared me half to death."

I helped gather up the Pyrex baking dish, thankful it didn't break. I checked under the aluminum wrapper. Its contents seemed in order.

"It's all sloshed around." Memaw peeked inside before I fixed the aluminum back onto the dish.

"It's spaghetti casserole," I said. "I think it'll be okay."

"Are these for me?" In the hubbub I'd dropped the flowers.

"Who else would they be for?" I handed her the flowers, pressing the casserole dish one-handed into my side.

"I did tell you Avett would be there tonight," she remarked. Still, she was flattered by the gesture. I deemed it best not to tell her they'd been left in the shop.

"They're for you," I told her. "For all we know, Avett will bring a date of her own." It was true. Memaw *had* told me that Avett would be at the book club meeting tonight. But that information had played only a small part in convincing me to go with her.

Memaw smiled a smile I'd gotten used to over the last thirty years. A smile with her whole head. Her lips, cheeks, eyes, and even ears got involved, going pink at the edges.

"I'll just put these in water, and we'll be ready to go."

She retreated to the kitchen. In her foyer was a large piece of furniture my Pawpaw had built, a hall tree. There was nothing but her small purse, hanging alone on the hook to the right side. "What about the book?" I called out to her.

"Oh, right, that."

Memaw searched her bedroom and finally came out with the paperback copy of the book I'd ordered for her. The spine looked pristine. *Did she even read it?* Book club, for Memaw, was a social event more than anything else. I didn't say a word.

We were outside on the porch when she owned up to it herself. "I just couldn't get into this one," she said, holding the book up. "Too much murder and not enough anything else. I want characters. I want romance. I want it all."

"It has that," I replied. "You just have to get past the first three chapters. But I agree with you—they *were* pretty grim."

"You think she'll notice? I mean, if I have her sign it..."

Memaw jiggled the backdoor of the car open for me. I placed the casserole on the floorboard. My hands were still hot. It must've *just* come out of the oven.

"I doubt Pam will notice," I told Memaw. "She'll probably think you bought a brand new copy especially for the signature. If anything, she'll be impressed."

Memaw nodded happily. Then she scooted into the passenger seat of the Volkswagen Golf. They were both about equal height.

The author, Pam Isley, was attending this week's meeting. She was the main reason I'd agreed to attend. Her first series, The Dog Woofed, including the titles The Dog Woofed Murder, The Dog Woofed Poison, and eight others, were some of mine and my mother's favorite books. I'd read them in middle school after coming across the first few on the bookshelf in our living room.

It turned out Pam Isley had bought a penthouse condo across the bay on Gaiman Island. The island was a place a number of rich older people, snowbirds, called home at least half of the year.

Pam was staying there to work on her next book. Fitting Memaw's little book club into her schedule for a reading and a book signing hadn't been difficult.

This new book was a thriller, not a cozy little mystery like The Dog Woofed. But I liked the way it started. The protagonist was a veteran of the War on Terror turned private eye. He and his new assistant tracked down a killer who'd been picking off members of a well-to-do family. Not to ruin it but the killer was a member of the family—a bastard son.

Perhaps my opinions were skewed a bit. I'd spent some time in the military, six years in the Air Force right after high school. Then I used the GI Bill to fund my education in business.

Like the protagonist, I'd gone out on my own after that. My grandfather, Pawpaw, had left me just enough money to open a coffee shop here in Niilhaasi. Kapow Koffee served locally roasted coffee, cold brew, and espresso drinks. It was also the only comic book shop in a seventy mile radius.

When I'd found out about Pam's upcoming visit to the book club, I phoned my mom in Costa Rica—my parents had moved there shortly before Pawpaw's passing.

"That's all right. We'll be home for Thanksgiving," Mom had assured me. Despite Pam being one of her favorite authors, I couldn't talk her into flying back here for the meeting.

We got into the car. I put the clutch to the floor and turned the key. The diesel engine of my small Volkswagen thrummed to life.

"Kirby, you don't think she'll recognize you, will she?"

"Recognize me?"

"You know," Memaw whispered like we weren't the only two people in the car, "with the murder. These author types —I bet she's looking for inspiration for her next book. She probably wants to pick your brain."

"How would she even know I'd be coming tonight?" I asked. "This is *your* book club. Maybe she wants to pick *your* brain. Forty years of paralegal work—maybe it's you she's after." I winked.

Memaw shook her head, laughing. "You're right. I was just thinking it's an odd coincidence. She buys a house here after those terrible murders..."

She didn't need to remind me. I was accused of the first murder. It had been staged to look like it happened in my shop. And the victim was my co-owner and best friend, Ryan Walker.

"That's not what I heard." I shifted gears. "I heard she bought the place years ago, but this is the first time she's used it."

"Well, I just know I don't want to get too close to her," Memaw said. "Those first two chapters made my skin crawl."

"Haven't you always told me wait before making any rash decisions? Why don't we meet her? Then we can decide. Besides, it's not like her buying a house all the way across the bay is going to have any effect on us."

2

"Fancy seeing you here." Avett wandered toward me from the other side of the potluck table, a big grin on her face.

I was just taking the aluminum foil off of Memaw's spaghetti casserole. The odd assortment of foods on the table was rivaled only by the array of guests. The Elks Lodge parking lot had never been so full.

"I *could* say the same to you," I said. But, of course, that was a lie. I'd known for several days that Avett would be here.

"Aunt Barb said you might come." She smiled again. "Long time no see. How's my favorite red-headed barista?"

I absentmindedly put my hand to my head. "It's more copper than red—the color of an old penny."

"Pennies are mostly made of zinc these days."

"Hence why I said old. And I'm good, by the way. Great, actually. You look well." Avett looked more than well. She looked as gorgeous as ever. Tall and brunette. Her honey brown eyes gave the table a once over.

"So what do you think?" she asked, pointing to the food.

I grimaced playfully. "It looks, um... edible?"

"Yep," she agreed. "Edible. I think that's the best way to describe it. In fact, I might wait and get something *after* the meeting. Are you a fan of Mo's Hideaway?"

"Are you kidding? Of course I am. Who doesn't like pizza?" Over the past couple of weeks, I'd actually run through scenarios like this one in my head. I'd practiced what I'd say to her, try to explain why I hadn't called or texted over the past couple of months, and then do my best to remedy the situation, and finish by asking her out. Now here I was, the one being asked out. At least that's what it seemed like.

"Would you maybe want to go? That is, with me, after?" she asked.

Yeah, this was going a lot better than I'd imagined it would. I hadn't had to bumble over my speech about work being crazy—which it was.

"I'd love to," I answered her hurriedly.

"It's a date," she said. Then she went to correct. "I mean, it, uh—"

"A date?" I offered. This time I was the one smiling.

We'd done it once before—date, that is. Well, we went on *one* date. It had ended abruptly when my friend Felicia barged into the coffee shop with news about Ryan's murder investigation.

It was that news, or maybe Felicia, that scared Avett off. After, Avett had friended me on Facebook. But in the months since, I never really felt like there was a good opportunity to ask her out again. I was busy most nights at the shop. And the nights I wasn't, I was usually helping Memaw out around her house—or letting her take me to dinner at our favorite restaurant, The Fish Camp.

"Riiight," Avett said. "A date. I'll have to let Aunt Barb know I won't be riding home with her."

Her smile, which was already wide—ruby red lips and perfectly white teeth—grew broader. She lifted up on her tiptoes and looked around the room, not finding her aunt in the sea of blue-haired women attending tonight's club meeting.

"So, Kirby, why are you here—really? Are you a big mystery fan?"

"Just a bit," I confided. "*The Dog Woofed* is up there on my list of favorite books. I read them ages ago."

"Seriously?" Avett giggled.

"Yeah—what's wrong with that?"

"Nothing's *wrong* with that. I just love those books. I thought I was the only one. But I see now," she gestured to the crowd, "I was mistaken. Which book is your favorite? I think I've read all eleven, maybe three or four times apiece."

"Eleven?" I was surprised.

Avett's eyes went wide. "You haven't read book eleven —*The Dog Woofed Premeditation*?"

"No." I shook my head. "I haven't."

"That's right!" Avett sucked in a breath through her teeth— she was bless your hearting me. "Pam only released it a couple of years ago. It was her first book after like ten years away. It really tied everything up. Sad news about Cleatus though..."

"Don't tell me." I put my hand up. "No spoilers."

Cleatus was the dog who starred in the series. Or rather, he was Clementine Griffith's dog. Clementine, the protagonist, was up there with Nancy Drew and The Hardy Boys in my book.

"All right," Avett said. "I'll try not to give anything away. But I was planning to ask her a few things tonight. The new book is *just* okay. I'd much rather be reading more Clem and Cleatus. Wouldn't you?"

"Well, *I've* got one more book to read," I retorted.

"True that. Here." She grabbed my hand. "Let's find a seat."

But before we could do that, Avett's aunt, Barbara Simone, joined us. She had a paper plate loaded carefully with select food items. None of which were touching. And Memaw's casserole hadn't made the cut.

"Good evening, Kirby." Her voice was that of a stern elementary school principal. The severe look of Professor McGonagall, from the Harry Potter books, came to mind.

"Aunt Barb," Avett said, her smile never faltering, "Kirby and I were about to get a seat."

"You two aren't going to eat?" It was an accusation as much as it was a question.

"About that..."

Avett informed her aunt about her plans for the rest of the evening.

A moment later, another woman, this one also around Memaw and Barb's age—somewhere between sixty and late seventies—tapped Barb on the shoulder.

"Barbara, is that you?"

It seemed an excellent time to leave, to find those seats, but Avett lingered there another moment. I wondered why until I got a better look at the woman.

If you added twenty or so years to the author's photo at the back of *The Dog Woofed* books, put some gray in with the blonde shoulder length hair, and stamped crows feet to the side of her large circular glasses, well, then you would have Pam Isley.

And somehow Pam Isley knew Avett's Aunt Barb.

"Pamela—it's so good to see you," Barb said. They

hugged awkwardly, like Barb was afraid of getting her blouse wrinkled. "Oh, and let me introduce you to my niece, Avett, and this is her friend, Kirby. They don't usually come to these meetings. But *you* have drawn a fair few people out of the woodwork."

Barb glanced around the Elks meeting room testily. This wasn't the book club she'd signed up for—the one typically made up of twelve to fifteen old women who gossiped more words a week than they read.

Avett shot her arm out toward Pam. "It's so good to meet you. When Aunt Barb told me she knew you from college... Well, I never expected you to actually accept the invitation."

So Avett set this whole thing up? That made sense.

"Oh, dear, it's nothing. I needed to get away from it all. There's nothing quite like the Florida coast in the fall. It's like a season unto itself. Not too cold, not too hot. I love it here."

Briefly, I wondered if we'd been experiencing the same climate. There was still sweat inching down my sleeve.

"Kirby, here, is also a big fan," Avett said. "He was just telling me how much he loved the eleventh book, *The Dog Woofed Premeditation.*" Avett's mischievous smile made me want to step on the toe of her pointed pump. "Tell me again, what was your favorite part?"

"Loved it," I lied and stuck out my own hand for her to shake. "And I'll tell you later. Pam doesn't want to be bothered with that."

Pam seemed to agree. "Oh, they're silly books, aren't they? Sometimes you fall in love with a character and you can't keep from writing them."

"Or reading them," Avett put in.

"Right." Pam scrunched her nose playfully. Then she eyed the potluck. "I better find a snack. I hate reading on an empty stomach. It was good seeing you, Barb. Make sure I get you a signed copy of the book. Where *is* Kelly Sue?"

We all gave Pam quizzical looks.

"Sorry," she said. "My assistant. I don't know what I'd do without her. If only she'd stop disappearing."

As if on command, a bright eyed young woman with vivid red hair manifested from behind Avett. She was about a head shorter than Avett which explained why we hadn't seen her until now. The girl handed Pam a paper plate. Much unlike Barb's, the food was crammed together, touching. It looked as if she'd taken a bit of everything and put it on the plate—even Memaw's spaghetti casserole.

"I was making you a plate," Kelly Sue said.

"You see what I mean. The girl is a godsend. Anyway," Pam said, "I'm looking forward to our discussion. I didn't know I had so many fans in Florida."

"It was nice meeting you," Avett said. We left Barb there with Pam and Kelly Sue. Avett tugged at my arm, giving me another mischievous look. And she proceeded to giggle as we made our way to two empty seats.

Memaw smiled at me from across the room. She was in cahoots with her friend Gail. I could tell they were talking about me—about us. Setting me up with Avett was number one on Memaw's agenda for the evening.

Check.

A few minutes later, Barb brought the meeting to order. She held up Pam's latest book—the thriller—*Death of the Family*. They briefly went through talking points on it before introducing Pam up to the podium. She read a passage from an untitled and yet-to-be-published second thriller. Then she fielded questions. Mostly from Avett.

After the book club meeting, and Pam's book signing, Avett and I slipped away on our own. Memaw had exactly no trouble finding a ride home with her friend Gail. In fact, she actually insisted I leave her there. The original book club members stayed behind, cleaning up, ensuring the Elks Lodge was even more pristine than when they'd unlocked the doors that evening.

Avett and I walked hand-in-hand to the car. It was like we were starting off exactly where we'd left things on our first date. Those months between the two meant nothing to either of us. As a single, thirty-year-old adult, I'd come to understand just how hard dating could be after high school. Avett had her own troubled past, an abusive ex-husband that she'd left in Atlanta.

We parked in the front of my shop, picked up Gambit, my dachshund, and took him on the short walk over to Mo's Hideaway.

Unlike Kapow Koffee, which was now over a year old, Mo's Hideaway had been a mainstay of Main Street for going on twenty years. We ate in the secluded alley that served as their outside dining.

Gambit liked Avett. I mean, who wouldn't? She never spent more than five minutes between scratches behind his ears. And I was ninety-five percent sure she had slipped the dapple-haired dachshund a piece of crust under the table.

We walked him back to the shop and I was halfway inside, turning on lights, when Avett said, "You aren't going to take me home?"

So, that's it. Date over.

"Of course I am," I replied. It wasn't as if I thought we were going upstairs to my studio apartment. I just wasn't ready for the date to be over.

Just guessing, but I figured Avett's trepidations stemmed

from the last time I'd invited her into the shop—when my longtime friend, Felicia Strong, and the detective who handled Ryan's murder investigation, intruded on us. I thought there might be some sort of animosity between the two women.

"I just thought," I trailed off.

"You thought what?" Avett asked, smiling.

I shrugged.

"Well, whatever you thought, you didn't know I have an early shift tomorrow." Avett stooped down. This time Gambit flipped over and gave her his belly to rub. "It was good seeing you, too," she told him.

Back in the car. Back with her fingers laced over mine on the gear shift. I put the car into reverse and eased out onto Main Street. "So, where to?"

"You know where my Aunt Barb lives?"

I nodded.

"That's where."

"Really?" I was surprised. "I didn't know you *lived* with your aunt. I mean, I knew you moved here to be close to her. I just thought you'd, ya know, have a place of your own."

"Says the guy who lives above his coffee shop and eats dinner with his grandmother every week."

"Hey!" I playfully retorted. "At least I have my own place."

We both laughed.

"No," she said, sighing. "Really, I didn't plan on staying with her so long. But I think she likes me there. It helps for her not to be alone. And every time I talk about moving out, she makes several good points. She wants me to save for a down payment on a house instead of waste my money on rent."

"I understand that. Let's see. I'll be able to afford a house in ten, fifteen years tops."

Avett snickered. "Honestly, I've had the money for a month or so. I just can't find the right house. Aunt Barb's even more picky. She's found something wrong with every one I've showed her. For now, I've just stopped looking."

"Still, it's really nice of her to let you stay like that."

"I'm sure Memaw would do the same for you."

"She would," I agreed. "But I'm not really into sharing a bathroom. Something about seeing your roommate's dentures and Poligrip on the counter all the time just doesn't sit right with me."

"Thank God for separate bathrooms."

"When I stayed the night there a few months back—I accidentally put the Poligrip on my toothbrush. They *do* know it looks exactly like a toothpaste tube, don't they?"

Avett roared with laughter.

"It's not funny," I protested.

The car idled in neutral in her aunt's driveway. I didn't want to be presumptuous and pull the parking brake. But I did hope for a kiss. This was one of those times where a more suave guy would say something better than, "I had a really nice time tonight." But that wasn't me.

"Do you want to come in?" she asked. "Not for a nightcap or anything," she added at the surprised look I gave her. "It's just, I could loan you that book—the last Dog Woofed."

"Yeah." The parking brake *zipped* as I yanked it up. "Sounds good. You're sure Barb won't mind?"

"She's much more laid back than she comes off," Avett assured me. "Okay, that's not true. But she's fine. I promise. She's probably in bed by now."

"You mean she doesn't wait up?" I joked.

"Thankfully, no. She does, however, give my mother progress reports. Lucky for me, my mom is fifteen years her junior and a lot more progressive."

We made it under the front porch light when Avett stopped me with a hand gesture. "Let me poke my head in and make sure Aunt Barb's not out in her nightgown. She'd never forgive me if you saw her in it. Oh, and let me give you this."

Avett inched closer, puckered her lips, and we kissed a brief but pleasant kiss. We'd shared a similar encounter on our first date. I'd spent far too many nights thinking about it. This one solidified things—Avett was an excellent kisser.

It's those perfect lips, I thought to myself.

"Be right back," she told me.

But Avett *didn't* come right back.

Instead, she called to me from inside. "Oh my God, Kirby. Get in here. I think... I think she's dead."

3

I rushed inside, my heart thudding in my chest. No way was this happening again. Surely Avett was mistaken.

Barb's living room was old fashioned. Hard and uncomfortable furniture was pushed neatly toward each wall, leaving the room open. It was dimly lit by the light of a ceiling fan—one whose chain made a clinking sound as it connected with the light fixture on each rotation of the blade. Those were the only sounds in the room aside from Avett's sobs. She was crumpled on the floor, her back against an antique couch, several feet away from her aunt's body.

An Oriental rug covered most of the tile floor. On it, Barb Simone's frail body lay in a small heap, her legs bent in toward her chest. One hand was clenched over her stomach while the other was raised as if to catch her fall.

There was no outward sign of trauma. No blood. But she was white as a ghost, her skin almost transparent, wrinkled, with liver spots and blue veins standing out in relief. And she *had* already changed into her nightgown and slippers.

"There's no pulse," Avett mumbled.

I pulled Avett up and away onto the couch.

"It's okay," I told her. Knowing it wasn't.

This was two—the second body I'd happened across. It didn't make it any easier than the first time.

"Shouldn't you, uh..." Words failed me. I realized that Avett, being a nurse, should be better suited in a situation like this. Better suited than me. But maybe the shock of the situation had thrown her off her game.

"Do CPR?" she offered.

"Yeah, that."

She shook her head. A tear fell down her cheek. Then she sniffled into my shoulder. "No. Aunt Barb has a DNR—a do-not-resuscitate order," she said when I looked confused at the acronym. "You know she's had bouts of cancer, right?"

It was my turn to shake my head. I didn't. Memaw, much unlike Barb Simone, wasn't one to gossip. She had no reason to tell me about Barb's illnesses. So she hadn't.

"We really thought she had it beat this last time." Avett took a deep breath. "I guess not..."

"I'll call 911," I told her.

"Thank you." Her voice was a whisper. A look of shock and disbelief etched her face.

Things went a lot differently than the last time I called *that* number.

The fire department was the first to arrive, not the police. An ambulance came next. And finally, a couple of uniformed officers appeared on the scene. They took a few photos and statements from both Avett and me.

The ordeal only lasted a couple of hours. They pronounced Barb's death, assumed natural causes, and about thirty minutes later someone else showed up. And it *wasn't* our county's medical examiner. No, I recognized Chuck Dickson immediately. He had graduated high school the same year as my mom, and my folks had him over throughout the years. He was co-owner of Dickson and O'Neil Funeral Home.

He asked a few similar questions, but it seemed that Barb had already set up most everything with Chuck several years earlier. He asked if there was anything he could do for Avett, anyone he should call. He had Barb's daughter listed as a contact, but Avett assured him that she would make that one. He took the body, and that was that.

When it all was done, I was there with Avett—she was now alone in her aunt's house. It felt surreal. I started to wonder if I'd overstayed my welcome but knew better than to leave her by herself after something of this magnitude.

There had to be something I could do to help her.

"Do you want me to make us some tea?" I asked.

She looked up at me guiltily, checking the cuckoo clock on the wall behind me. "It's late. Do you need to go? What time does the shop open?"

"I'm fine." I said, not uttering the words, "6:30 a.m." I pushed back the knowledge that Fridays were always the busiest at the shop. Then I put my hand over her balled fist. "Unless you want me to go..."

"No." She shook her head vigorously. "I'm tired. But I don't think I can sleep. Tea sounds nice."

In the kitchen, I found a kettle and the Yerba Mate tea that Avett drank instead of coffee. How I was going to make a relationship with a non-coffee drinker work, I didn't know. All I knew was I liked her. A lot. Next to the Yerba Mate was a can of chamomile.

"The chamomile," she said before I asked.

The good thing about kettles is they boil despite being

watched. In only a few minutes, we had mugs of tea with a few scoops of sugar apiece. I handed her the drink and sat down across the kitchen table. Like the kitchen, it was small —cozy—and at least thirty years out of date. The oven and the refrigerator were avocado, if you can call that a color. The microwave sat out on the counter. It wasn't installed in the cabinetry.

"I didn't realize Barb had health problems," I said, slurping the scalding hot tea. It burned the tip of my tongue. Of course, even at a time like this, I was going to be myself. *Especially at a time like this*, I thought disparagingly.

"I don't know what I said before," Avett confided. "It wasn't like Aunt Barb to show any weakness. She wore wigs and didn't go out of the house when the chemo was really rough. I doubt even your Memaw knows about the cancer."

"Ah," was the best reaction I could muster.

"I guess this is just what happens with time." Avett took a sip from her own mug. "We all get frail. I just—I didn't see this coming. You know? Aunt Barb was like a rock. She was sturdy."

I nodded. I did know.

"Sorry," Avett said. "My emotions are a bit up and down right now. Until what—six months ago—Aunt Barb was someone I saw on holidays. Or in the summer—when she came to Atlanta to visit my mom. They weren't close."

Avett leaned back in her chair. " I remember I took her to the Coke Museum once. She didn't even try anything. That's how she was. Not a risk taker."

I nodded, understanding.

"Then she invited me here after the divorce. Since then we've gotten along really well. I'll miss her. Now I'm the one who has to call everyone—my mom, her daughter. It just feels odd... Like I'm not supposed to be the one to deliver this kind of news. My cousin, Holly—have you ever met her?"

"Maybe once or twice," I said. Barb's daughter was about ten years my senior..

Avett nodded absentmindedly. "She lives outside New Orleans. Do you think I should call now? It's so late..."

"I think I'd want to know."

"Yeah. Me, too. Do you mind staying while I make the calls?"

"Not at all," I said. "But I'll give you some privacy. Where's the bathroom?"

She pointed down the hall. "There's one just in the hallway. Or you could use Aunt Barb's. It's in her room... with the Poligrip."

Even in her darkest moments, she was able to sprinkle in some humor.

"I'll pass," I said.

Her grin faded. "You know. Now I have to use the little girl's room too. I'll make the calls after."

We retreated to the separate facilities. I was in the middle of washing my hands when her voice penetrated the door between us. "Kirby," she said hesitantly. "There's something I want you to see."

"It's not Poligrip, is it?" I tried to lighten the mood.

She shook her head and led me through Barb's room and into the master bath. Avett pointed into the toilet. "Vomit," she said.

"Yours?"

"No. Aunt Barb's. Did the police come back here?"

I shrugged. "I'm not sure."

Avett bit her lip. "Maybe it was food poisoning? She *was* clutching her stomach, wasn't she?"

"She was."

Avett flushed the toilet. "Okay... I don't know if it matters. But I'll call and let the police know. Maybe someone from the health department follows up on things like this. I'm trying to think, what did she eat today?"

"Potluck," I reminded her. "I wonder if anyone else got sick."

"I hope not," Avett said.

Back in the kitchen, Avett paced the cramped room. She recounted the story several times for Barb's daughter, for her mother—Barb's sister—and for a few other relatives that I didn't catch the names of.

She ended the last call with a weary sigh.

"Thank you *so much* for staying. I know it wasn't exactly how you pictured the evening ending. I seriously don't know what I would've done without the support."

"It's no problem," I said. "Just let me know how I can help. Okay?"

"Well, for starters, I think I'm ready for bed. Holly will be here tomorrow. I'll let you know if anything else comes up." Exhaustion had replaced the grief and shock on her face. I didn't feel like a spring chicken either. Avett ushered me out with a peck on my cheek. "Thanks again."

4

After only a few hours of sleep, exhaustion was plastered to my face in the form of dark circles beneath my eyes. Lucky for me, I happened to own a coffee shop. A good one, too.

With several shots of espresso to fuel me, I managed to open the store, ten minutes late.

No one noticed.

Everything was quiet for the first five minutes or so. That is, aside from Gambit's snoring. The dachshund was curled up in his dog bed. It sat at the foot of a glass display cabinet filled with the week's new edition of comic books.

"I hope you're sleeping for the both of us," I told him.

It took a while but I was coming to terms with the fact that I'd become one of those dog owners who talked to their pet. Part of me was still dealing with being a dog owner. Not that I didn't love dogs—or Gambit. It was just he'd been Ryan's dog. And Ryan was gone. The dachshund had helped to solve Ryan's murder. And now I thought of him as more than a pet—a friend, a co-owner, and the shop's mascot.

Gambit didn't reply. He continued his snooze as I made a

thermos full of our dark roast coffee. I sipped on a cup of it while I waited for the regulars to arrive.

It was Friday after all—our busiest day—the shop would be packed in a matter of hours.

I drained the cup and went to fix another when the bell on the door jingled. The first customer had arrived. I turned back and an all too familiar face greeted me from the door. Felicia was still gleaming with sweat from the morning's CrossFit workout.

"And where were you?" she asked, stalking to the counter with mock condemnation. "You know you're gonna have to run eventually. You can't skip out every time one's scheduled."

"I'm pretty sure I can," I retorted. "But, no, it wasn't because of the run. I had kind of a late night last night. Did you hear about Barb Simone?"

"I did." Felicia nodded. "But I didn't realize... I mean... you were there?"

"I was."

"Why?" she asked. "Were you with Memaw or something?"

I shook my head. I mean, she'd find out eventually. Felicia was a detective. Getting answers was her job description.

"I was on a date," I said.

"Oh." She seemed to lose the wind from her sails. "So you're dating what's her name again?"

"Her name is Avett," I reminded her. "And no. I mean, maybe? I don't know. It was just a second date. Or maybe, a second first date. We got to chatting at book club last night, then went out for pizza after."

"Then you found Barb..."

"She did."

"So, you like what—walked her to the door?" Felicia asked speculatively. I wasn't sure if this was her in cop mode, asking about the incident, or if this was her questioning my relationship status.

"Yeah... I walked her to the door." This jogged my memory. "Actually, she was supposed to loan me a book. I guess I'll have to buy it on Amazon—like a normal person."

"We also have a library," Felicia remarked.

"Right. Good idea," I said. But I was distracted by the reminder there was another Dog Woofed book that I hadn't read. *Yet.*

I started her coffee. I made two shots of espresso, pumped chocolate syrup at the bottom of a cup, and began to froth some milk.

"Well, it's a shame about Barb," Felicia stated. "And I'm really sorry you had to be there for that. I'm sure that didn't feel good. It probably brought up some bad memories, huh? I'm here if you need to talk. You know that, right?"

"I know that." She sounded like she my sister, not my friend, and not the girl I'd had a crush on since high school. I'd recently learned that she might've felt the same—back then, not now. In those days, we'd been especially good friends. The type that liked our friendship so much that we didn't chance ruining it by revealing our true feelings for one another.

Our lives had taken separate paths. I had joined the Air Force, gotten engaged, broke off said engagement, and moved back here. She had graduated college, gotten married, had a little girl, and got divorced.

Her job as a lead detective for the Niilhaasi Police Department was how we'd crossed paths again. We hadn't spoken in ten years when Ryan's murder thrust us back into each other's lives. Now Felicia was a morning regular. And sometimes I went to work out at the CrossFit box with her beforehand. We chatted a few minutes every morning five days a week. Plus, we exchanged phone calls and a text or two pretty regularly. Most were just funny GIFs—things we knew the other would get a kick out of.

I passed her coffee across the counter, and Felicia took a sip. She looked at me as if something had occurred to her. "Since when do you go to book club? I thought that was Memaw's thing."

"It is," I agreed. "But there was a special event last night. A guest author. Have you heard of Pam Isley?"

"Are you serious? *The Dog Woofed*? I love those books. You do know I'm a mystery buff. I picked those up in college and devoured every one. I still read a book or two a week."

"That doesn't go away when it's your job?" I asked.

"No, most definitely not." Felicia took a sip of her mocha. "In fact, it's a nice escape. I don't often deal with cases that are *real* mysteries. Most are straightforward. Does Pam have a new book out?"

"Yeah. A new book. A thriller. I mean, unless you're like me..."

Felicia raised an inquisitive eyebrow.

"Oh," I shrugged, "I didn't know that there's an eleventh Dog Woofed book, *The Dog Woofed Premeditation*. That's the book Avett was *supposed* to loan me."

"An eleventh book? Really? I don't remember reading it. Forget about the library," she told me. "I'll beat you there— just like I *would've* beat you on the run this morning."

"I'm not disputing that." I put my hands up in surrender, a gesture Felicia was probably used to.

I waved to her as she left. Her conversation had stirred up more than the memory of that book. There was someone

I'd neglected to talk to, and she wasn't going to be pleased if she heard last night's story from anyone else.

"Crap! Memaw," I said loudly enough to wake Gambit.

I pulled out my phone and dialed.

Memaw called three times and texted several more in the hours since that first phone call. And Memaw *never* texted. She was taking Barb's loss hard. But that wasn't unexpected. Since Pawpaw's death, she had spoken of him often. His memory was a presence in our every conversation.

I texted her back.

I'll go with you tonight after work. Avett says they won't mind the company.
Holly just got in.

After hitting send, I gave the shop a quick once over. Everything looked in order. The regulars were nestled into their booths, laptops open, mugs of steaming coffee to keep them company. There was no line, not another customer in sight. I deemed it a good time to take Gambit for a short walk.

He thought so too. He'd been prancing underneath my feet for the last ten minutes. A clear indication he wanted something. And seeing his dog dish and water bowl full, I knew what that something was.

Behind the shop was a narrow alley just spacious enough for a garbage truck to fit inside, empty our dumpster, and back out again. Like every other dumpster in the world, ours reeked.

I attempted to scoot Gambit past it toward 1st Avenue. But the stubborn dachshund wasn't having it. He crouched low—well, lower—being a dachshund he was already quite low to the ground. Then he growled gutturally, his lip curling in a snarl.

"Oh, no, what've you found?" I poked my head around the dumpster, cringing. I was sure there'd be a rat scurrying around behind it, or possibly something worse—like a dead body.

What I found was much better. A cat peered up at me with green eyes. It had a white spot on its chest but was otherwise black. After taking me and Gambit in for a moment, it jetted between my legs and across the alley.

Gambit's reflexes weren't at all what he wished for them to be. The cat was well away by the time he started his run. But if his reflexes were bad, mine were even worse. The jerk of the leash caught me off guard. It went slipping out my hand. Gambit took off after the cat.

I caught up to him on the next street. He had tried to take a shortcut around a corner and his leash had gotten stuck in a fence.

The cat was nowhere to be seen. Gambit huffed all the way back, turning back every few minutes in hopes of finding the cat.

When we returned to the shop there was someone else there to greet us. Felicia had returned. And in addition to her plainclothes cop attire, she wore a smirk on her face.

"I saw you finally getting in that run," she said, laughing.

"Yeah, well, this numbskull," I gestured to Gambit, "had to chase after a cat."

"Oh, Gambit," she cooed. "Were you trying to protect Kirby from the evil kitty?"

Gambit, who loved baby talk, padded up to her. Then he jumped up on his hind legs, placing his front paws on Felicia's knees, stretching. She scratched his ears.

"Do you want another mocha?" I asked. It was a rare occasion to see Felicia twice in one day. I was surprised she wasn't with her partner, Detective Ross.

"Is the sky blue? Do birds sing?" A new poster on the other side of the shop caught her eye. "Is the Captain Marvel movie going to kick butt? You bet I want another mocha. But I'm here to bring you this."

I hadn't paid attention to the counter beside her. Felicia had already laid a thick book down on top of it, beside the cash register. It had that library binding sheen, but I could read the title. *The Dog Woofed Premeditation.*

"They had two copies. And because I know the head librarian, Sabrina, so well I was able to get her to make you your very own library card."

"All you needed was my driver's license, huh..."

"And where would I get your driver's license?" She tapped on her chin, feigning being lost in thought. "It's not as if I work for local law enforcement... Oh wait. I do."

"Thanks," I said. I picked up the book and perused the back cover.

Felicia bent down. "I know," she baby talked again, "it's like Kirby forgot I have a job to do and can't stay here and play all day."

That was my cue to start her coffee.

"How's Memaw doing?" she asked after the loud sound of me frothing the milk died away.

"Not good," I answered honestly. "This has been a bit of a shock. She's texted me all morning. *Texted.* It's mostly in all caps. I'm not sure if she's yelling or just hitting the wrong buttons."

"She probably can't see the words unless the caps lock is on. My grandpa does that." Felicia tucked a strand of curly hair behind her ear, but even more of it fell out of place. Her hair was the only part of Felicia's appearance that didn't scream "slick detective." It was an unruly mess of tight curls. "And how about your *friend*, Avett? How's she taking her aunt's death?"

"We haven't spoken much. Just texts—without caps lock. I think she's doing all right. But I'll find out in a couple hours. Memaw wants to take food over there and see Holly, Barb's daughter."

Felicia nodded.

"Give them both my best."

I passed Felicia's mocha across the counter. She sipped it in parting. Gambit followed her to the door.

"Gosh. I love this dog," she said. She gave him one last pat on the head and was gone.

It would take several more minutes—hours—for my opinion of him to return to normal. I wasn't ready to forgive him for the cat escapade. Not yet.

5

"Okay. You're forgiven," I told the dachshund as he clambered into the car. He didn't seem to care. The afternoon's cat chase was behind him. He was excited to partake in another of his favorite pastimes, riding in the car.

Gambit wasn't the typical canine passenger. He didn't poke his head out the window and let his tongue hang to the side. No, he didn't like for the window to be rolled down period. Instead, he kept his nose as close to the passenger side A/C vent as was possible—essentially licking up the cold air as soon as it was pushed out for him.

The drive to Memaw's was a short one. There was a new housing development coming in just before her street. The houses there were closely packed together with hardly a tree between them, a stark contrast to the tall pines and oaks that lined Memaw's drive.

"You're early," she said in lieu of a greeting.

"I texted you I was on my way," I said to her from the front door, wiping my feet.

"Oh, Kirby," she said. "You know I can't read your texts. I just send 'em. Who's working at the shop?"

"I left it in Sarah's capable hands."

My assistant manager, Sarah, was a big reason that things at the shop were going so well. A tall blonde in her senior year of college, or rather, she should be in her senior year. She'd decided to take some time off from college to pursue her dream of writing. Working at Kapow Koffee was just a means to an end. But she did it well, organizing the comic book side of the shop so that it, too, was profitable. There were gaming nights every month, Facebook marketing campaigns, and a dozen other avenues that helped the community of Niilhaasi see the shop in a whole new light.

I probably owed Sarah another raise.

Memaw craned her neck around the corner to the kitchen. "Oh, well that's good," she said. "Sarah's very capable. Now come help me in the kitchen."

I unclipped Gambit from his leash and did as I was told. He went about his usual business of sniffing the house, checking if anything had changed in the few days since his last visit. Knowing Memaw, nothing had.

But then I sniffed. Something smelled wonderful.

When I rounded the corner to the kitchen, I came to a sudden stop at the view of older lady rear side. Memaw was leaning down, peering inside the oven.

"What's the occasion?" I asked.

Memaw scooted a pan of homemade macaroni and cheese halfway out of the oven with a barely there oven mitt —how she didn't burn her fingers was beyond me. "I'd say it needs another minute. But I'm always paranoid with this broiler."

The cheese and the bread crumbs on top weren't to that

level of crisp I was used to seeing, but it still looked fit enough to eat. This was one of Memaw's signature dishes, one reserved for occasions like Thanksgiving and Christmas. It wasn't meant for our Friday evening dinners, that much was for sure. She shoved it back in the oven.

"I thought we could take this to Barb's with us. I'm sure Holly and her kids are in need of a good meal. And your friend, Avett." Memaw winked. "She could use a little meat on her bones, herself."

"I told her we were coming over after we ate. She was going to order pizza for the kids."

"Y'all had that last night," Memaw argued.

"I know. That's why she's getting it for the kids. She didn't say anything about her and Holly."

"That's good. They can eat this."

When Memaw pulled it out this time, the edges were brown, almost, but not quite burnt. She yanked a foot or so of aluminum foil off the roll and crinkled it on top. And she was ready to go.

"Right, right now? Is it okay if Gambit stays here?" I asked her.

"Oh, he can come along. I'm sure Holly's kids would love to have a playmate."

"Not if they're anything like Barb," I murmured under my breath. Memaw's friend had not been too fond of Gambit. He seemed to feel likewise. In their last meeting, he'd nipped at her heels.

Two days in a row, I was loading food into the back floorboard of the car. I managed to get the blistering hot mac and cheese inside while Memaw and the dog slipped into the front seat together. He perched on her lap, ready to lick up the freon cooled air.

Ten minutes later, we pulled into Barb's driveway

behind a minivan. It sat alongside Avett's purple coupe. Two other vehicles were parked half on the road and half on Barb's immaculately kept grass. A flowerbed bordered the house, its flowers still in bloom even this late in the year.

"She always had a green thumb," Memaw observed. "You know, she even mowed this grass herself. There's a gas push mower sitting in that garage. You'd never see me touch one of those things."

This I knew was true. I'd been cutting Memaw's grass since the day I'd moved back to town. Thankfully, not with a push mower. Pawpaw had left a suitable John Deere riding mower in their backyard shed.

"So, who else is here?" I pointed to the cars by the road.

"Well, that one is Gail's Cadillac. The other, I'm not sure."

Memaw knocked lightly on the door. I expected Avett to answer, but expectations don't often meet with reality. A boy, around ten years old, opened the door wide.

"It's more of Grandma's friends," he murmured, probably not loud enough for anyone inside to hear. Then he sank his face to a tablet held tightly with both hands and did an about face.

We followed him inside. He knew his way around the house enough not to bump into the walls. His thumbs swept back and forth as he played a video game on his device.

"Oh, Martha, how are you?" Barb's daughter, Holly, skirted the boy.

Holly wrapped Memaw in a tight hug while I stood behind them with the still piping hot dish in my grasp and Gambit's leash around my wrist. The dog wound it between my legs, circling me.

"Seriously?" I grumbled. I wasn't looking to have two

leash mishaps in one day. I maneuvered to let the leash fall, and the dachshund bolted between the women.

He found someone he knew he liked. Avett bent down to scratch Gambit's ears before she tiptoed just behind the two women and relieved me of the mac and cheese dish with a peck on my cheek.

"You're never going to guess who's here," she whispered as I followed her down the hall, back to the all too familiar kitchen.

Just her tone made it an easy guess. It was the exact same tone she'd taken when discussing Pam Isley the night before. And sure enough, Pam sat at the cramped kitchen table. Her assistant, Kelly Sue, with hair the color of flames, leaned on the counter behind her. They both held coffee mugs.

Avett put the mac and cheese down on the stovetop next to an assortment of other dishes. These looked like the remnants of last night's book club meeting—likely brought over by Memaw's friend, Gail, whose chirpy voice could be heard prattling away in the living room.

I guessed rightly that Memaw and Holly had fallen into her trap after hearing there stifled "uh huh's" at the tail-end of Gail's sentences. Gail never let anyone get a word in edgewise.

"Now, you're gonna have to remind me your name," Pam said to me from the table. "I admit I'm terrible with them."

"Kirby."

"Kirby," Pam Isley repeated. "Well, Kirby, we were just discussing Barbara. As you can imagine, her death came as somewhat of a shock. After all, we'd seen her just last night."

I wondered how Pam and her assistant came to learn about Barb's death. While word of mouth spreads quickly in a small town like Niilhaasi, Pam was staying over on Gaiman Island. There, the news traveled at his own pace—a slow one.

"We were just coming over to bring her a few extra signed books. Ya know, just in case she wanted to give them as gifts or something." Kelly Sue indicated a stack of books on the kitchen counter. And there was my answer. They hadn't known about Barb. At least not until they'd gotten here.

"You know," Avett mused. "Aunt Barb was pretty tight-lipped about your friendship in college. How *exactly* did you two know each other?" She sat down next to Pam and found her mug of tea.

Avett perked up as Pam began to answer.

"We were sorority sisters. Barb and I were roommates at the house. Here, I brought a few photos with me. We found them cleaning up the house in Vermont. I thought Barb would like to see them.

"Kelly Sue, could you hand me that first book?"

Pam leafed through the book, found the photos, and passed them across the table to Avett. I stretched over her to get a view of them. The pictures were faded, their colors lost, making them a monochromatic yellowish brown.

"Here's one of all three of us. There's me, and there's Barb, and Dori."

Dori? Doreen? Who's Doreen? Avett seemed to know—or she didn't want to be rude and ask. Being on the periphery of the conversation, I decided not to ask. The name *was* familiar, although I couldn't place it.

"Here. This is one of my favorites. See, there's Doreen with Barb and Cyrus."

The picture was of two women. They had the hippie look of the late 60s or early 70s. I couldn't tell the difference.

Their hair was long. They both could've been blonde, or the photo was just that faded and washed out. Where Pam's finger rested there was a dog, a Labrador—just like Cleatus from her books.

"Cyrus?" Avett questioned.

"Barb's lab, of course." Pam nodded. "Don't tell me she never mentioned Cyrus."

"I didn't think she was much of a dog person," I chimed in.

"No?" Pam scoffed. "You're kidding, aren't you?" She looked from me to Avett, who shrugged apologetically, and back again.

I shrugged, too, but out of habit. I *wasn't* kidding.

"Not a dog person..." Pam shook her head slowly. "Why Cleatus and Clementine were modeled after Barb and Cyrus. You must know *that*, right?"

Avett's jaw dropped. Mine too.

I had trouble picturing Barb Simone as a dog person— in fact, my mind wouldn't allow it. Trying to picture the stern older woman I knew as the carefree young sleuth Clementine, well that was plain out of the question. Clem was one of my favorite fictional characters. She wasn't—she couldn't be—Barb Simone.

Even looking at these old photos, it was hard to connect the beautiful maybe-blonde girl with her aged counterpart. I mean, sure, I did see the resemblance in the nose and the long neck. But the road from this photo to the Barb I'd known was a long and winding one.

"You've got to be kidding," Avett finally found her voice. "Aunt Barb never... She knew I loved these books. She never —never said a—"

"I'm not kidding you in the slightest," Pam asserted. "Why would I lie about a thing like this? I didn't say any of the stories are true. But the characters... Well, they're very much based on these two." Her finger pressed back down onto the photograph.

"Why would she keep that a secret?" Avett turned to me. "What do *you* think?"

"I'm not sure," I said, unsure. Avett's Aunt Barb wasn't known for keeping secrets—quite the opposite, actually. She was the town gossip. But much like the cancer thing, she never divulged much about herself. She had been interested in other people's problems.

"I might know why," Pam said softly. "It comes down to Doreen. She and Barb were the closest in college. In fact, most of the time I was the third wheel in *their* adventures. I think maybe when they lost touch—maybe she put this all behind her. They had a bit of a falling out, you see. And Barb would've wanted to forget it all."

"Where's Doreen now?" I asked. The name still rang some bells somewhere in the back of my mind.

Kelly Sue huffed from the other side of the counter. We were the only two standing. "Doreen died several years ago," she said. "It's a painful memory."

"It's quite all right," Pam said. "No harm done. Actually, if these two don't know about Cyrus, then I have an excellent story to tell."

"You do?" Kelly Sue asked.

"It's one you haven't heard either," Pam said.

"I'm all ears." Avett took a sip of tea, then leaned closer to Pam.

The author cocked her head toward me. "I'd love to hear it."

Pam smiled thinly, took a sip of her coffee, and cleared her throat.

6

"It was our sophomore year. All three of us lived in the sorority house. Like I said, Barb was my roommate, and Dori was her best friend in the world. We studied together, went to football games—even went out on group dates together. That sort of thing.

"Like most sorority houses, we had a sorority mother. Her name was Mrs. Margaret. She was an alumna, a sister like us, but around thirty years our senior. Her husband had died on Normandy, and she never remarried. Instead, she took the job as housemother. She wasn't mean. She was strict. A devout Catholic and a rule follower. I'm sure you know the type..."

She sounded a lot like Barb—but I kept that comment to myself.

"Well, one day," Pam went on, "we were driving off campus, goofing off. I forget where or why. But we came across a dog in the road. We almost hit him. Barb swerved. Her car ended up in the brambles on the side of the road.

"The dog just stood there in the middle of the road and waited for us to get out. He acted as if we were the ones being stupid. He had no collar or tag. He seemed to like us, especially Barb. We couldn't just leave him there. Dori and I had to help push the car back out onto the road. Then Barb had the idea to let the dog inside the car.

"We were *supposed* to find him a home, take him to a shelter, or something like that."

Pam paused to take a sip of tea.

"Well, it soon became apparent we were doing nothing of the sort. Barb headed straight for the sorority house.

"'He just needs some water and to get cleaned up,' she told us. And we believed her—if you believe that. We helped her sneak that pup up to the second floor. We got him fed and cleaned up. Then I remember I said, 'Okay, Barb, now what?' And then she said, 'What do you mean, now what?'"

"Did you really keep him?" Avett asked.

"We did." Pam said with a nod. "The first day or two I thought for sure we would end up taking him to the pound. But Barb would say things like 'tomorrow, I promise' and I would believe her.

"I kind of wished we'd get caught by Mrs. Margaret. I had trouble with lying to her. But Cyrus, Barb had named him by then, was as quiet as a mouse. He didn't whine or bark or anything like that. We used the back stairwell to let him outside. Mrs. Margaret hardly ever used it. And I think the other house staff thought it was funny. God knows all the girls did."

"She didn't find out—Mrs. Margaret—did she?" Avett was caught up in the story, hanging on every one of Pam's words.

"Oh, she did eventually. There was one time early on when she stepped in his poop in the yard. Dori convinced her that it was black bear feces. Said she'd seen one digging in our trash. That frightened Mrs. Margaret so much she didn't go outside for weeks."

"But what happened when she found out?" Kelly Sue was also enthralled with the story. I guess I was too. But I still had trouble picturing it. Barb, our Barb, young and breaking the rules. The inspiration for my all-time favorite sleuth.

"It was almost a year later," Pam said. "By that time she knew something was amiss, although she didn't know what. She started searching our rooms. Finally, she found Cyrus hiding under the bed. She almost had a heart attack. Then we told her how long he'd been there. And she almost had another.

"The funny thing is, Mrs. Margaret was a softy at heart. She didn't think it was right to put him out on the street after all that—after a year of keeping him under her nose."

"So she let you keep him?" Kelly Sue acted surprised.

"She did." Pam nodded.

"He really never barked?" I asked skeptically. Gambit was used to people. But he barked at the sound of thunder. *And at the sight of a cat*, I reminded myself.

Pam gave me an interested look. "I thought you said you read the books."

"I did," I said, defensive.

"Then you know Cleatus only woofs when there's trouble afoot. Same could be said for Cyrus. He barked when there was trouble."

"Like what kind of trouble?" Avett asked.

"Just the usual sorority kind—boys climbing into windows, girls climbing out of windows." Pam looked up thoughtfully. "There was one time..."

"One time, what?" Avett leaned even closer.

"You ever hear of the Romeo Strangler?" Pam asked us.

We all shook our heads no.

"Not really your high profile serial killer. He only killed once. This was at a sorority house at another school. See, at the time the papers had all blown it out of proportion. It was nothing like that Ted Bundy several years later.

"There was a statewide hunt for the killer. They knew who he was, and that he had skipped town. Like good little sorority girls, we all heard stories—or made some up—about sightings around *our* campus."

Pam took a sip of tea. All three of us were quiet. The house itself wasn't. The chatter of Gail with Memaw and Holly came to us from the living room. Gambit had found a playmate in Holly's little girl. A ball bounced down the hall, and he skidded after it, his nails *tap-tapping* on the tile floor.

Pam cleared her throat. "On every Sunday afternoon we had a social event where fraternity boys were allowed over. They were only allowed on the first floor, of course, in the common areas and such. However, this didn't stop some girls from trying their luck.

"On one Sunday, I remember Barb needing to go upstairs for a book. She came running back to the stairwell, waving frantically at Dori and me to come upstairs. This was before Mrs. Margaret had found the dog.

"'Cyrus is acting up,' she told us. 'Come see.'"

"Sure enough, the dog was whining. He scratched at our door. He even barked. We didn't know what to do. We couldn't let him out, not with the house full of the boys downstairs. Mrs. Margaret roamed the place like a warden on those days. We were sure to get caught.

"'Let's see if he'll tinkle in the shower,' I remember Dori suggested. It seemed as good an idea as any. Barb grabbed Cyrus's collar. I inched the door open and checked the hall.

"But with the door open, Cyrus put his full weight into

getting loose and Barb lost her hold. He went sprinting down the hallway. We thought we were goners. Surely, he would be seen."

"What happened?" Avett pressed.

"He went to the end of the hall and scratched on Alice Marble's door," Pam said. "He had a low growl. It was the first and only time I remember hearing it. We rushed to the door, and it was locked. That didn't stop *our* Barb, now, did it? She took a bobby pin from her hair, twisted it in the lock, and opened the door without questioning Cyrus's strange behavior in the slightest."

"The Romeo Strangler was in the room with Alice Marble?" Kelly Sue guessed.

"Alice's face was purple. The strangler was already to her window by the time we came crashing through the door. He fell and injured himself trying to get away.

"In all the commotion afterward, Barb was able to get Cyrus back to the room before Mrs. Margaret made it upstairs. The police had no trouble finding the strangler after that. And Alice Marble didn't dare speak a word about Cyrus to anyone not in the know, not even the police."

"She owed him her life," I said.

I couldn't help but think of Gambit. While he wasn't able to save Ryan's life, he did do his part in uncovering Ryan's murderer.

In that moment, he stopped chasing the ball and peered at us from down the hall. Then he traipsed toward me, tail wagging furiously.

"Who do we have here?" Pam bent down and offered her hand for him to sniff. Gambit enjoyed the attention. He arched his long back in a regal fashion.

"This is Gambit," Avett told her. "Kirby's dog."

"Well, he sure is handsome," Pam eyed me, "kind of like you. Tell me, Avett, are the two of you dating?"

My heart stopped a moment, then Avett smiled and nodded. "We are," she said, meeting my eyes.

~

So, what does a guy do after he finds out he's dating one of the most beautiful women in town? Some may wonder, *how does he spend the rest of his Friday night?*

Well, if he's me, he gets a to go order of amberjack, gouda cheese grits, and coleslaw from The Fish Camp, a local eatery specializing in fresh Gulf seafood. Then he meets a crew of weirdos that he calls friends at Kapow Koffee for a game of Dungeons and Dragons.

In fairness, both Memaw and Avett were understanding about it. This meeting had been on the books for a long time—and it was about more than just a game.

Tim Grayson and his son Damian were waiting outside the shop. I'd only truly gotten to know them both after Ryan's death. Tim owned Niilhaasi's local computer repair shop, Doc's IT Dock. It was a play on words—doc as in doctor, but also dock as computer docking station and the shop was down on the edge of the harbor, literally on the dock of the bay.

Damian, Tim's son, was a senior in high school. He had to be one of the brightest kids I'd ever met. His mind was like a steel trap, remembering almost every fact it ever came across.

Corey, our last player, pulled up. The lights of his yellow Corvette streamed inside as I dimmed the house lights to an acceptable level—just enough to read our character sheets by. It was cavelike enough for the right ambiance.

Corey hadn't always played with the group—I hadn't either. I replaced Ryan while Corey replaced Marc Drake. Marc, Ryan's killer, was now serving a life sentence without any chance of parole.

The four of us chatted for a bit before the game. I made coffee for myself and Damian. Corey and Tim threw back a couple of beers. They offered condolences, then made several inappropriate jokes in regard to finding such a body while on a date.

It was an odd sort of night that way. We never said it, but I could tell we were all thinking about Ryan.

"So, what about Felicia?" Corey finally asked.

"Yeah, what about Felicia?" Damian smiled. He was a bright kid, but also a bit of a smart ass.

"Uh... we're just friends," I answered. I hoped they'd leave it at that.

They didn't.

"*Just* friends?" Corey raised an eyebrow.

"Come on, guys," I pleaded. "You know it's complicated. She has a kid. She has a job with long hours—an ex-husband I've never seen eye-to-eye with. And parents that don't like me. The list goes on from there."

"Sounds like a "cop" out." Damian did finger quotes.

"Which is funny because she is a cop," Corey said, smiling at his failed addition to the joke.

"And the winner of the worst joke of the night award goes to you two."

"If it makes a difference," Tim butted in, "I'm with them. You should've at least asked that Felicia girl out. I mean, when you had the chance."

"Okay," I said. "That settles it."

"Settles what?" Damian asked skeptically.

"Sorry," I answered him. "My internal monologue... But

did I mention next week's campaign is cancelled? I've actually got a date that night."

"No!" Tim argued. "You can't be serious."

"I can. And I am."

While Avett and I didn't actually have a date planned, I was bent on rectifying that situation as soon as these three jerks left the premises.

I saw them out, texted Avett, and then something else caught my eye. The book.

"Come on, Gambit," I said, sliding the library book from the edge of the counter. "It's bedtime."

He followed me upstairs and wedged himself beside me in bed. He groaned in protest about every ten minutes. I'd lied to him. Bedtime meant the light should be off. And I didn't turn off the light for several hours.

7

P recisely at 8:00 a.m, and with tired eyes from two nights lack of sleep, I grudgingly opened the shop. Another day of work stood between me and a day of much needed rest.

It was a dreary morning—the first indication that winter was approaching. The clouds had rolled in thick over the bay and the temp was barely seventy. Although my weather app assured me it would be back up in the eighties by the weekend.

The gross weather meant that people would stay home that morning and make their own coffee. This was bad for business. Saturdays were usually my busiest day.

But I had around half of Pam's book left to finish. And no distractions.

The shop was eerily quiet. Aside from the small dribble of rain on the sidewalk outside, there was only the low hum of the music on the sound system.

Gambit pressed his eyes closed tight in what I assumed was his doggy way of convincing his bladder he didn't have to go outside. I'd tried to make him go twice. But two times he'd stood his ground under the awning at the door of the shop, refusing to step out into the drizzle.

Out there now was a young woman beneath an umbrella. She closed it and then shook it out. When she stepped inside, I recognized her.

Kelly Sue looked around, giving the place a once over. She smiled at me and approached the counter.

"Hi," I gave her a friendly smile. "Kelly Sue, right?"

She nodded. "And you're Kirby. You know," she said, gesturing around, "this place is way better than you described it. I kind of pictured a dank old comic book shop with a Keurig. *Fifty cents for a cup of coffee. Put it in the bucket.*" That last part was a bit, sort of like she was a standup comic on stage.

"No," she continued. "This is a coffee shop. Yeah, you have some comics and action figures on display. But the smell of this place." She sniffed the air. "This is what I've been after. Before today, I was driving all the way out to the Starbucks—all the way to the outlets. That's almost two hours out and back I could've been writing. Everything changes today."

"You write too?" I asked her, a little surprised.

"I do." She looked away sheepishly, finding it easier to look at the ground than meet my eyes. "I know it's cliché. But that's why I wanted to work with Pam. I wanted to be on the inside of the publishing madness. Plus, internships at publishing houses are hard to come by. Pam needed an assistant. I jumped on it."

"How long have you worked with her?"

Kelly Sue's eyes bored deeper into the floor. "Six years," she said, her voice shrinking. "I know it's crazy, right? It's a long time to be an assistant. But in the long run though, it's paying off. I *did* get a book deal. That's actually what I'm working on, finishing up another round of edits. My book comes out fall of next year."

"So you're like a year away," I said.

"Don't say it like that," she weakly protested. "If you say it like that, I'll get all mopey, and procrastinate. It's hard enough not to get depressed with the weather all dreary outside."

She didn't have to say that twice.

"Sorry," I apologized. But she'd piqued my interest. "Do you mind if I ask what genre you write? Is it mystery?"

"Mystery. Thriller. A little bit family drama. A little bit literary—cause, ya know, why not?"

"So, kind of like Pam's last book, *Death of the Family*?"

"A lot like it." Kelly Sue averted her eyes once more. She smiled, shaking her head. "What did you think of it, really? You're a big fan of Pam's work, aren't you? I do see you're reading her last book."

"Yeah. I am." Embarrassed, I scooted the book off the counter. And I wondered if this conversation would get back to Pam. If she was the type of author to react to every review —even the ones told to her assistant in a coffee shop. Which reminded me—

"Hey, can I take your order real quick?"

"Oh, yeah, of course... I'll take a large Americano with room."

I rang up the order, then moved down to the espresso machine to make her drink. I thought a moment. *What should I say? The truth? Or something like the truth?* I opted for the latter.

"I, uh, I liked the book. It just wasn't *The Dog Woofed*. I love *The Dog Woofed*."

"I can see that." She laughed.

"I guess I'm more of a cozy fan," I said. "All those intense moments—they make me want to put the book down. I mean, I understand for other readers that's what makes them turn the pages. Not me."

"I get it."

"You want this for here, right?" I gestured at the shots of espresso. She nodded, and I found one of our oversized mugs, the kind that needs two hands—or incredible wrist strength—to take the first few sips.

Kelly Sue absentmindedly glanced behind her as if checking for something outside.

"Where is Pam?" I asked her. "Do you get time off to write, or how does that work?"

"Something like that." She shrugged. "This is *our* writing time. Pam likes to be around books when she's writing. She's usually at the library. It's a bit eccentric, but she prefers that to home. And like I said, I've been driving all the way to Starbucks because I prefer people. And a drink like this." She took the mug in both hands. "Now, I better get back to the writing, er, editing."

Kelly Sue added some half and half to the coffee. Then she slipped into a booth on the other side of the partition that ran down the line of booths in the center of the room. Every now and then, I saw the top of her head bob up above it. The faint click of her keyboard was almost lost. The dreary weather outside kept most everyone at home through the morning.

It wasn't until after lunchtime, and well after Kelly Sue left, that business picked up.

It allowed me ample time that morning to sneak away behind the counter and read. But nowhere near enough to finish the book.

8

I still had a quarter of the book left to finish when a gaggle of customers herded into the shop. The sun had poked its head out, and the book sat on the counter distracting me. I wasn't going to get more pages in soon.

Even in muggy Florida, where the fall season is more a notion than a reality, people lose it for anything pumpkin spice. I squinted at my dwindling supply of syrup, thinking maybe it was time to put a special on caramel apple lattes. There were at least two bottles of apple flavoring and probably enough caramel in stock to make lattes for a football team.

I scribbled the special down on a small chalkboard beside the cash register.

And speaking of football teams, I'd learned that the Niilhaasi Tigers might actually have a team this year. The mayor himself had called and asked for us to take part in the upcoming homecoming parade. Sarah would be throwing candy from a float while I manned the shop. The route went straight down Main Street, just outside the door.

I had high hopes the extra traffic would bring in a few new customers. A couple of coffees later and they might become *loyal* customers. Not that we weren't garnering a few of those already. Along with, or perhaps because of Sarah's marketing efforts, each month we'd steadily grown the business. I looked out at the familiar faces seated in the booths between the counter and the window wall.

A timer beside me *beeped*.

"There's hot coffee brewed if anyone wants a refill," I called out to them. Saturdays were the day to be generous with both time and coffee.

I sighed inwardly after filling the last cup of the onslaught. With the line gone, I went to pick up the book. But one last glance up at the windowed door told me not to bother. Two familiar individuals caught my eye. One took long sure strides while the other struggled to keep up. The little girl got distracted and stopped, and then her mother tugged her by the arm.

Felicia was still scolding her when the two of them veered inside.

"You've got to pay attention where you're going. What if we're out in the street? What if a car was coming?"

"Mom!" Neena whined. "We were on the sidewalk. I *knew* we were on the sidewalk. I just wanted to look in the scrapbook store."

"Uh huh, sure." Felicia nodded. "I remember what happened when we tried to scrapbook. You picked out all the stuff. And I did all the work."

"I promise I—"

"Can we just get coffee right now? We'll talk about broken promises and scrapbooks later."

Neena's head drooped down to her shoulders. She wasn't defeated. The battle was put on hold.

"Kids." Felicia sighed. She smiled up at me, rolling her eyes out of Neena's view.

Should've asked Felicia out. The worlds popped into my head.

Those guys had a way of getting under my skin. I couldn't explain it. They were like the friends I never wanted. But I wound up with them, and they were here to stay. The four of us shared a bond that would last a lifetime.

"The usual?" I asked.

"For me, yes." Felicia looked down at her daughter in question.

"Um... Can I have a caramel apple latte?"

Score.

"Definitely," I said. "And let me guess—extra caramel?"

Neena grinned in excitement, eliciting another roll of the eyes from Felicia. This one the girl caught. "Hey!" she retorted. "You do you. I like caramel."

Aroused by the sudden uproar, Gambit decided to let his presence be known. He stood up from the comforts of his doggy bed and gave himself a shake. The sound of his collar jingling rang across the shop. He trotted over to them.

Neena plopped onto the floor. She gave him some scratches behind the ears before asking him in her most energetic voice—which was saying something, "Where's your ball?"

Gambit's tail began to flutter like he might take off. He searched the shop for his prized faded yellow tennis ball. When he had trouble finding it, I pointed him in the right direction.

"Gambit," I motioned, "there it is."

He scampered under Karen's table. A regular, Karen casually moved her feet. For whatever reason, she was working on Saturday. But she wasn't in her usual work attire, opting for a pair of yoga pants and a tank top.

Gambit brought the ball over near Neena, but he wouldn't hand it over without a bit of a scuffle. Neena then threw it the length of the shop.

"The way things are going," Felicia said to me, "I'm going to have to get her one."

"A dog?" I asked. Finished frothing, I poured the milk into to go cups for each latte.

"Yeah, a dog." Felicia grumbled. "It's actually why I'm here today..."

I looked at her about as apprehensively as she was looking at me.

"Don't be mad," she said, which increased my apprehension. "You remember I told you about Dr. Capullo, the medical examiner?"

I nodded. It was hard to forget. He'd been one of the key reasons my status as a suspect in Ryan's murder was dropped.

"Well, he lives a few houses down from my parents. And he has a dachshund. Well, his wife has a dachshund. Neena's been going over to play with it."

"Interesting," I said slowly, still unsure where this was going. But knowing Felicia as long as I had, I knew it was going somewhere.

"A *girl* dachshund." Felicia offered a playful grimace. "I notice Gambit's, ya know—well let's just say Ryan didn't heed Bob Barker's advice. Dr. Capullo's wife, Meera, wants to breed her—she's a retired champion. They're looking for a stud. Your name *might* have popped up."

"It might've?"

"Okay. It *did* come up. And it turns out the vet has Gambit's genetic information on file."

"What did you sign me up for? I don't have Gambit's papers or anything."

"It's a doggy playdate," she said. "Nothing formal or anything. Just show up tomorrow morning, say 9:30, at the dog park. Do you think you can do that?"

"Felicia," I moaned. "Why? Why'd you have to go and ruin my perfect Sunday?"

"Perfect Sunday." She rolled her eyes, this time at me. "What'd you have planned—nothing?"

"That was exactly what I had planned. Seriously—there has to be someone else with a dachshund around here."

"But not that one," she said. "I've told you before, I love Gambit. And Neena, she wants a puppy."

"A few months ago a dog was off the table—I remember you saying as much."

"That was a few months ago." Felicia shrugged like there was more to the story. I could tell by her look that something had changed. And it wasn't necessarily a good thing.

"What's changed?" I pressed.

She glanced at Neena, still playing with Gambit, and lowered her voice. "Derek's moving," she whispered. "He took a job. In Dallas—of all places—freaking half the continent away. We haven't told Neena yet. But things are going to get a lot more complicated. She'll see him in the summer, for Christmas holidays, that kind of thing. I'm so scared that her life is going to be turned upside down."

"A puppy's not going to solve that."

"No, you're right, it's not. But it'll help. Just think about it. Dr. Capullo will be at the park tomorrow whether you show up or not. I'll let him know you're a maybe. Plus, it's not like Gambit has to do any real work. When he's done his thing, he might as well be in Dallas."

I handed her the two lattes.

Gambit watched longingly as they left.

When he trotted back toward the counter, I asked him, "What has Felicia gotten us into?"

That evening was again spent at Barb's house with Avett and Memaw. But there was no Pam Isley—or the chittering of Gail.

Avett found a couple of board games in the hall closet. We ate Chinese takeout and played Clue with Holly's kids, Carolina and Chase, while Memaw and Holly rummaged through Barb's closet to pick out Barb's burial attire. The funeral wasn't scheduled until Monday.

We had played two games and were well into a third when Holly wandered into the kitchen to scrounge for more food.

"Holly Brubaker. In the kitchen. With the butter knife," Chase chortled. My own suspicions were shifting from Colonel Mustard to Professor Plum.

Holly went for the leftover fried rice, but she stood at the refrigerator idly for a moment.

"We probably should get rid of this food," Holly said to Avett. "They're only going to be bringing more over. And we're out of your hair Tuesday."

"I'll take care of it," Avett replied.

"We'll take care of it," I said, offering my services.

"Can't it wait for this game?" Carolina pleaded. "I think I know who did it."

It turned out Carolina did not know. It was Professor Plum, but I'd made a mistake on his choice of weapon. Avett won the game.

The kids meandered toward the television, allowing us grownups to clean up both the game and the fridge.

We chucked out everything, most of it in tin pans. But a few dishes were in Tupperware and needed to be washed and returned to Gail.

"Oh my gosh. What is this stuff?" Avett removed the last lid.

I laughed at her. "You're from Georgia," I said flatly. "You *really* don't know what that is?"

Avett scrunched up her nose at me. "Just because I'm from the South doesn't mean I eat everything I see at a family reunion. I mean, I've *seen* this dish before. But I've never gone so far as to eat it—or to ask whomever made it what the heck it was. Please, will you do me this honor? What is this abomination?"

"Pear salad." I inspected it more closely. The water from the pears had all seeped out to the bottom of the container. But the mayonnaise and cheese concoction still maintained an edible facade. Something was missing. "That's odd," I said.

"What's odd?" Avett asked before sliding the contents of the dish into the trash can, water and all.

"Those don't have cherries," I answered. "The one on Pam's plate the other night—it had cherries."

"It did. You're right." Avett nodded. "Do you think maybe there was another tray? One with. One without. You know how those gals like to throw a party. They get crazy."

"Maybe," I said slowly.

But something didn't sit right in the back of my mind. Before I could put my finger on what it was, Memaw called loudly from Barb's bedroom.

"Kirby," she yelled. "Would you see to your dog? He keeps coming back here. We don't have time to play."

"Sure," I said. "Hold on."

I went out to the garage to throw away the trash. Then I beckoned Gambit to follow me to Barb's den where Avett and I settled on a movie to watch with the kids. I scooped the dog off the ground and plopped him into my lap.

"Such a good boy." Avett went nose to nose with him, embracing the puppy snuggles.

I still wasn't sure if I wanted to take him to the park the next day. It all seemed kind of weird to me. I mean, I know it's natural. How else would you get more dachshunds in the world? *Maybe from a breeder*, I thought.

Still. It felt weird.

The tipping point came a little while later—I made the mistake of telling Avett about it. She was of the same persuasion as Felicia. And she all but said she wanted a dachshund puppy of her own.

9

W ith Avett's convincing still in the back of my mind the next morning, I found myself trudging behind Gambit as he pranced regally down the sidewalk. He acted as if he knew what was about to happen. This was a far cry from our first trip to the park, in which Gambit stubbornly tried to yank me back to the shop for the entirety of the half mile walk.

We'd been enough times now that he knew the way. He was fond of the dog park's ample amount of space for ball chasing, another favorite pastime—after snoozing in his dog bed and riding in the car.

To my surprise, Dr. Capullo was ten minutes early. I had expected him to bring his wife. But it was just the two of them, Dr. Capullo and his dog. The smooth-haired miniature dachshund was as red and coppery as a brand new penny. Her coat shone in the midmorning sun. She was energetic, already sprinting to and fro in the enclosed space.

"Kirby, right?" he said.

"Yeah."

Dr. Capullo wore a long sleeve button-down shirt with the sleeves rolled up to the elbows. He had on khaki shorts and a pair of brown loafers. His hair was black, graying around his temples. With his clean-cut appearance, expensive wristwatch, and overall demeanor, there was no doubting this man was a doctor.

"Scott Capullo," he said, reaching out his hand. "It's nice to finally meet you. Felicia's mentioned your name a few times now."

When I gave him a quizzical look, he laughed, saying, "All good things. I promise."

Like me, Gambit was wary. He wasn't sure what to make of the other dog. At first, he kept his distance. He stuck close to my ankles until I bent down and let him off the leash.

"Oh, and this is Cinderella," Dr. Capullo said.

Cinderella made the first move. She ventured over for the typical butt sniffing and playful chasing that dogs utilize to get to know each another.

Dr. Capullo pulled a blue racquetball from a pocket of his shorts, garnering both of the dogs' attentions. He threw it and they sprinted off after it, Gambit in the lead with Cinderella in hot pursuit.

"Sorry," he said. "Meera had to work today."

His wife, I assumed.

"Oh, okay." I nodded into the to go cup of coffee I'd brought along with me. I didn't press for any details. We shared an awkward moment of silence before the good doctor explained anyway.

"She's a cardiologist," he said. "And it's her turn for Sunday rounds at the hospital. As you can imagine, it's a highly coveted shift." He laughed at his own joke. "Really she's the lowest partner on the totem pole. Yeah, even doctors with their own practice get stuck doing things they don't want to do. I'm sure you can relate, owning your own business and all."

"I can," I agreed. "I've been doing the early morning shift since we opened—and there's no end in sight."

"Yuck." The doctor made a face. "I'm not much of a morning person myself. This is early for me on a Sunday. Meera woke me up when she was leaving."

Cinderella came trotting back triumphantly with the ball sticking halfway out of her mouth. She dropped it at Dr. Capullo's feet, then nudged it forward with her nose until he picked it up and threw it again.

Then he took a seat on a park bench under the feeble shade of a few pine trees. I did the same, giving him a few feet of man-space.

"Listen, Kirby," he said. "I want you to know that this *wasn't* my idea. It's just when Meera gets an idea in her head... well, you see what happens. It doesn't help that she already promised one to Neena—and thereby roped Felicia into this whole scheme. I don't think we'd even sell these puppies. You understand the position I'm in, don't you?"

"The one where you can't say no?" I offered.

"Exactly." He gave me a salute.

I smiled, telling him, "I'm all too familiar with that position. I got roped into mowing my grandmother's grass after this—and who knows what else. She's usually got a list."

He laughed through his nose. "Martha Jackson, right?"

"Right," I said. "Do you know her?"

"No. I just know of her. Mo, I mean Morris Grantley, her old boss, speaks highly of her. He's even been known to call his new paralegal Martha on occasion."

"New?" I scoffed. "Memaw's been for retired eight years."

"Some habits..." Dr. Capullo shrugged.

It figured that the district medical examiner would be on first name basis with the town's most high profile lawyer.

The dogs came back one more time—for one more throw. When they didn't return after a few minutes, well, I assumed they were getting to know each other better.

"And speaking of work," Dr. Capullo transitioned, "I hear you're pretty familiar with Barb Simone. You were there at the scene?"

"Yeah. I was..."

He nodded to himself. "See, Kirby, I'm typically involved in suspicious deaths. When someone like Barb reaches the end of their days, especially having an illness like cancer, well, it's usually up to their attending physician to sign the death certificate. The funeral home does the rest."

"Right," I said.

"But." He left the word hanging in the air for a second. "Holly, Barb's daughter, asked for an autopsy. See, Barb's oncologist had given her a clean bill of health not too long ago. And Holly didn't believe it could be cancer. She wanted to know *how* it happened."

He must've seen from my expression this came as news to me. "Right," he said. "I'm not even sure she told your friend Avett."

"She didn't mention it," I said.

Dr. Capullo shrugged. "I'm wondering if you noticed anything odd the other night?"

"There was." I thought back to it. "We, um, we found throw-up in her toilet. Oh, and she was clenching her fists to her stomach, her diaphragm."

"Those two things were actually documented," he said. "Thanks though. Man, I wish I knew what Barb ate that night."

"I can tell you that," I said, surprising him.

"You can?"

"Yeah. I was at the book club meeting. I saw her plate."

He pulled his phone from his pocket and brought up the Notes app. "Let's hear it."

I pictured Barb's plate, the way everything was spaced out away from the other food, then recounted what I remembered. "She had a couple of casseroles, green beans —that was probably a casserole as well—and a pear salad."

"A pear what?"

I smiled. "Sorry. This is two times in as many days I've had to explain this dish," I told him. "That's right, you're from Chicago or whatever."

"Detroit," he corrected.

"A pear salad," I said, "is basically just canned pear, mayonnaise, and shredded cheese. Oh, and sometimes a maraschino cherry on top. But Barb's didn't have one."

He laughed, but then stopped himself. "Wait... You're— you're serious?"

"Serious as the heart attacks they cause. I'm not really fond of them myself. But the gals of Memaw's generation, they love 'em."

"And that's who was there the night of book club?"

"That's who hosted it," I said. "But there were a lot of people there. They had a guest author do a reading."

"Interesting." Dr. Capullo pondered it. "Listen. I won't get the toxicology back for a few weeks, but I'll tell you this, Mrs. Simone didn't die of cancer. It was respiratory failure— some sort of poisoning."

The blood rushed from my face at the word poisoning. The hair on my neck prickled. I was reminded of *The Dog Woofed*. In the books, Clementine's ears would ring when she knew something from a premonition—before being told it. Usually, they rang when she suspected murder. Or when she found a clue. Was my body giving me the same sort of signals?

Was Barb murdered?

"Like food poisoning?" I asked him.

"Yes. And no," he said. "Food poisoning is usually a bacteria or a parasite. Not something toxic like this."

"What was it then? What does that mean?"

Dr. Capullo pressed his lips shut, then zipped his fingers on an imaginary zipper. "I've already said too much." He sighed. "You know, Felicia mentioned you have a habit of investigating mysteries. In fact, she probably said as much so I wouldn't tell you what I just did."

"It's not a habit if I've only done it once," I protested. "And in fairness, it was my best friend's murder. The one I was framed for... Thanks by the way."

Dr. Capullo had been the one to figure out that there was no way I committed the crime. He shrugged. "I was just doing my job."

The sun had crept higher in the sky and was angling above the thin pine trees around the park. Finally, the dogs made it back over to us.

Dr. Capullo stood and tucked the blue racquetball into his pocket. "Listen, Kirby, I'd appreciate it if you kept this conversation between us. We'll be in touch, all right? Hope I didn't keep you from your grandmother's grass too long. Man, the sun doesn't let up here, does it? I'm used to seasons —Florida only seems to have the one. Hot."

He attached a leash to Cinderella's collar.

At that moment, I wasn't concerned about grass. I wondered how I was supposed to keep this conversation to myself. How could I hide this knowledge from Avett—or from Memaw?

Dr. Capullo shook his head as if he was about to say something against his better judgment. "I guess you've probably put it together, haven't you? Well, you'd have this out soon enough anyway. Kirby, Barbara Simone was murdered."

10

Memaw had a glass of sweet tea waiting for me. She sat on the front porch swing, lazily pushing off with one foot. The other was propped up on the swing's armrest. Her Kindle was balanced on her slight belly with one hand, and she held her own glass of tea with the other.

"Now, that looks a lot better." She gestured at the yard. "If only we could get rid of those weeds—then it'd be something your Pawpaw would truly be proud of."

"I honestly don't think there's enough grass to do that," I said with a grin.

She smiled and set her Kindle down. I took a long sip of the cold tea. The outside air hovered in the lower eighties. But having spent the past hour or so in direct sunlight, my forehead was beaded with as much sweat as the condensation on the glass. And despite guzzling most of it, my mouth was still parched.

"I'll get you a refill," Memaw said. She slowly got out of the swing and was back only a few minutes later, Gambit trotting behind her. The dachshund had enjoyed the air conditioning while I was laboring outside.

It had given me time enough to think—to think long and hard about what Dr. Capullo said. I struggled with whether or not I should tell Memaw any of it. Of course, I knew she would eventually find out. But dealing this blow wasn't going to be easy.

I had mentally jotted down a list of suspects. And no, Memaw wasn't on that list. The problem was I wasn't overly confident that Memaw could keep this a secret for however long it needed to be kept. Her inner circle of friends operated sort of like half-witted spies with a few foreign agents interspersed in the mix. They covertly talked behind one another's backs until all news circulated to anyone and everyone within Niilhaasi's city limits and beyond.

"Kirb, is there something bothering you?" Memaw must've sensed my trepidation.

Did Dr. Capullo really expect me *not* to clue Memaw in? After all, she was one of Barb's closest friends. And her history working in law made her an excellent candidate to bounce ideas off of.

I reluctantly decided that I *should* tell Memaw. What she did with the information—that was up to her.

I sat down on the rocking chair opposite to the swing. It had been my Pawpaw's chair when he was alive, and it had seen better days. The weave on the seat was frayed; the armrests were worn. I was careful to watch for splinters.

"I guess you could say that," I told her. "I learned some troubling news this morning. It's about Barb."

"The viewing's tomorrow night," she said. "I understand if you don't want to come with me. After all, you've done so much already."

"No—no, it's not that."

"Well, good," she said. "You know I hate driving at night."

I smiled despite myself.

"What is it?" Memaw asked.

"What if I told you that Barb didn't die of cancer—what if it was something else?"

"That *would* be news," she said, nodding. "What was it?"

"What if I said she was poisoned?"

"Poisoned?" Memaw asked. "Poisoned how?"

"I don't really know," I said.

Memaw considered that. "Was it food poisoning? What a terrible accident..."

"Memaw," I said, "they don't think it was an accident."

"Preposterous," Memaw said for about the tenth time after I explained my conversation with Dr. Capullo. "There's no one who would have done such a thing. Your doctor friend is mistaken."

"I don't know. He seemed fairly confident." I knew Memaw would take it this way. She hadn't had time for it to circle inside her head like it had mine. And she wasn't there when we found Barb. She hadn't heard or seen everything at the book signing. The more things played out in my head, the more I was sure Dr. Capullo was right. Barb had been murdered. *But why?*

Memaw rocked her feet back but didn't let the swing move.

"Are you sure Barb didn't have any enemies?" It was the cheesiest, most clichéd line in any murder investigation. But it had to be asked.

"Enemies?" Memaw shook her head vehemently. "She didn't have enemies. This is silly talk."

"It's not. I'm just telling you what I know."

Memaw paused to take a sip of tea. "No. Barb didn't have enemies. If anything, she had rivals. You make it sound like she might've had this coming."

"No, Memaw," I protested. "I didn't mean for it to sound like that. I just mean she was the town gossip. I'm sure there has to be *someone* she offended."

"I'm sure there are plenty," Memaw agreed. "But no one would ever hurt her over something as a trivial as a rumor. And it's not like she was peddling lies. They were *all* true— and they would've gotten out eventually."

"Okay... Well, who were these rivals?" I asked.

"There're several." Memaw *hmmphed*. "Let's see. Nancy and Gail. Me... Am *I* on trial for murder?"

"No. No." I shook my head. "But Gail? Really?"

"Of course. There's not a woman in town Gail doesn't compete with in some way. You saw the other day she had to be the first over with food for the family."

"That's it," I said, standing. "The food."

"No. No, it's not it. She didn't cook most of it. It was leftovers from book club."

"I know," I said. "That's what I meant. I need to tell Dr. Capullo and Felicia about the food. Most of it is still sitting in Barb's trash can."

"You're barking up the wrong tree," Memaw said testily. "I bet it's that mystery writer. I told you she was here on false pretenses."

"You said she was here to interview me."

"Well I didn't know about her connection with Barb, now did I? If you ask me that's who the police should scrutinize."

I sighed. But it *did* sound plausible. In fact, we were probably all suspects in Felicia's eyes. Which brought up another good point—there was someone I needed to call.

11

Felicia picked up on the second ring. It was by far easier to start with her than work my way toward informing Avett—if Felicia would allow me.

"I know what you know," she answered. She sounded flustered already. "What do you want, Kirby?"

"A hello to start with," I said. "I hate when you go all bad cop on me." The truth was it reminded me of when she had suspected me of Ryan's murder.

"Yeah, well, I'm working on my off day," she said.

I tried to lighten the mood. "You don't think I make coffee on my day off?"

This was testing her patience, I knew. But I hoped that she would remember who she was talking to—one of her oldest friends.

Felicia sighed, easing up. I could feel her eyes roll on the other end of the line. "Kirby, what is it?"

"I just want to know what's going on."

"I already told you. I know what you know. Not much more."

"Barb was murdered?"

"Wait... Capullo told you that? I warned him not to tell you anything. We haven't formally opened the investigation."

"Then what are you doing at work today?" I asked pointedly.

"I'm doing our due diligence. Some background investigation. That's it. Police stuff. I'm not getting into it."

"We're already into it," I said.

She sighed. "Do you know how many murder investigations we do around here—aside from Ryan's?"

"I don't know, one or two—"

"Not even that many," she interjected.

"Okay," I said. "Barb was poisoned. We know that much."

"Thanks for the tip, Captain Obvious."

"No. Sorry. I'm getting to something." I took a breath. "What if I told you the food from the other night is at Barb's place right now? Would it be helpful for you to have that?"

"Kirby... where *is* this food you're talking about? And you're sure it's all from the book club meeting?"

"The trash," I said guiltily, then felt even more so when I said, "And it's mixed in with pizza and Chinese takeout."

"Wonderful," Felicia said. "Ross is over there now searching the place. It's the only place we have probable cause to search. That and the Elks Lodge, which was cleaned quite thoroughly. You don't know this because Avett doesn't have her phone."

"Is Avett in trouble?" I asked. I had to.

"Do you think your girlfriend did it?"

"That's not an answer to my question," I said.

"You're right. It's not. And you don't dispute she's your girlfriend? Are you guys official now? Are you going steady?"

"That's not funny," I told her.

"I know it's not," Felicia said. "It's just we have to look at everyone, especially someone as close to Barb as Avett. Were Avett and Barb on good terms?"

"The best." I said it without thinking. There were two people I knew weren't culpable of Barb's murder, and those two people were Memaw and Avett.

Gail, Pam Isley, heck, the assistant Kelly Sue, and half a dozen other women at that meeting were all on my list. But those two weren't. The notion that Felicia would even ask that question didn't sit well with me. It felt a lot like when I was sitting in the backseat of her unmarked car.

"She didn't do this," I said.

"Like I said, I'm just doing my due diligence. It's one of those things I *have* to ask. But in her defense, there isn't much she stood to gain from Barb's death. The house goes to the daughter. The other assets, too. And Ross says she hasn't done anything squirrelly—unless I count dating you."

"Ha." I wasn't laughing.

"Who else did Barb speak to that night? Did you see anyone touch her plate?"

"No," I said. "The food barely touched her plate. She talked to us, and to Pam, and to Pam's assistant."

"What's her name? Pam's assistant."

"Kelly Sue something-or-other."

I could hear Felicia's pencil scribbling in the background.

"Okay," she said. "Anything *else* come to mind?"

"No. Nothing really. Do you have any other leads?"

Felicia sighed. "Kirby, this isn't going to be like last time. I can't disclose anything to you—especially you being so close to Avett."

"Can you at least tell me how it happened?" I asked her. "How did Barb die?"

"I thought your friend, Dr. Capullo, told you."

"He just said poison."

"And that's all you need to know. Leave the detective work to me."

"Fine," I said.

"Fine," she said.

There was a second or two of dead air.

"Listen. I'm going to call your Memaw. And then I'm going to call it a day."

"All right," I said grudgingly.

"I'll see you tomorrow." She hung up before I could get another word in.

12

The funeral was a small affair. Most of Barb's family lived in Georgia; only some had made the short trek down. Memaw and her friends—including Gail—gathered together while I stuck as close to Avett as was possible. It was an awkward way to meet her family— her mom, her dad, and two sisters.

The shocking news of the murder made the event even more somber than it would've been anyway.

I noted that Barb's one time friend, Pam Isley, was a no show. Perhaps her celebrity prevented her from attending these types of things. *Or...* I dared not finish the thought.

"Leave the detective work to me." Felicia's words chimed in my head.

It was easier for me to spend the evening away from Avett. For all intents and purposes, she was cleared of suspicion. And she spent the evening with family, although some of them were now looking at her in the wrong light. Holly was ready for Avett to move out of her mother's place. There was already a for sale sign in the yard.

Gambit and I retreated to the upstairs flat. I still had

Pam's book to finish. I *thought* it would help to take my mind away from everything, but if anything, it made things worse.

I closed it a few hours later. My eyes were tired, but my mind was racing.

All in all, it *wasn't* a great book. I couldn't put my finger on why—why this one didn't live up to expectations? And more so, why did it matter? It was *just a book*—just a few hundred pages of words jumbled together, neatly telling a story.

Maybe it was the story itself that bothered me. The murder? *Maybe.* With Barb on my mind, that could very well be the reason.

But also, Pam had done an unforgivable thing. Something no author can get away with, not even one of Pam Isley's stature. She had *killed* the dog. I mean, not like with a murder. Cleatus had died of old age. But the scene was heartbreaking. It was a scene that anyone who had ever owned a dog could identify with—in an all too real way.

I thought about the dog I grew up with, Tilly. I vividly remembered her closing her eyes for the last time. My dad and I were alone in the room with the vet. The two of us cried our eyes out.

No, it wasn't the ending, I thought. It was something else.

I set the book on my nightstand and took a sip of water. Then I scratched Gambit on the top of his head, waking him up. His droopy left eye looked at me balefully and closed once again.

I decided to do the same. With the light out, I closed my eyes and waited for sleep to wash over me.

It didn't.

Instead, my brain churned with questions, going over the same things time and time again. I shut my eyes tighter in protest. This was the worst feeling. I'd had bouts of insomnia before. Back when Gwen and I had broken off our engagement. I'd sit up at night thinking about her, about the new guy she was with, and about every single mistake I'd made in our relationship.

It's not going to be like those nights, I told myself. I begged my brain to shut off.

It did. For a moment, I was sure I was asleep, or close to it. There was barely a thought in my head. The sound of Gambit's snores, and of my own breathing, were all that I heard.

Then my mind found its way back around to the book and to Pam Isley, recalling her stories from the other night —and her connection to Barb. There was something I wanted to know. The name Doreen—it had rung a bell. I'd meant to look into it but with all the other things going on, I'd forgotten.

I popped one eye open and felt for my phone on the nightstand.

From Wikipedia, the free encyclopedia

Pam Eleanor Isley (born August 5, 1944) is an American author of mystery and suspense novels. She is best known for her series *The Dog Woofed*. Each of the eleven novels in the series have been bestsellers and all remain in print.

Writing Career

Shortly after college, Pam moved to New York City with aspirations of working in journalism. She freelanced for several news outlets, finding time to write her debut novel, *The Dog Woofed Murder*, in her downtime between assignments. Two years later she published her second novel, *The Dog Woofed Poison*, and began writing fiction full-time.

Personal life

In 1980, Pam and her companion, Doreen, moved to a spacious farm in Vermont where they raised cows, chickens, and goats. Oddly, there was never a dog in the mix.

In September of 2009, the couple were among the first to wed when Vermont legalized same-sex marriage.

Doreen died in 2014 after a long illness.

Isley now splits her time between Vermont and a condo on the Florida Gulf Coast.

Published Works

- *The Dog Woofed Murder* (1974)
- *The Dog Woofed Poison* (1976)
- *The Dog Woofed Death* (1979)
- *The Dog Woofed Suicide* (1983)
- *The Dog Woofed Assassination* (1986)
- *The Dog Woofed Setup* (1991)
- *The Dog Woofed Strangulation* (1996)
- *The Dog Woofed Homicide* (1999)
- *The Dog Woofed Arsenic* (2002)
- *The Dog Woofed Conspiracy* (2004)
- *The Dog Woofed Premeditation* (2016)
- *Death of the Family* (2018)

13

I don't know why, but I thought for sure there'd be an answer as soon as the next day. In my mind, it was as simple as that. Felicia would do her job. And it would be over. Case solved.

At the gym, she ignored me during the warm up. Once we were out on a run, I tried to keep up, hoping I could ask her about the case.

"Any news?" I asked, already huffing for breath.

"None for you." She wasn't even winded. "But I'm happy you're here for a run."

"Well you didn't come in yesterday," I said.

"I know. That's because I didn't want to be badgered like I am right now. Did you miss your favorite customer?"

"You have to pay to be a customer," I told her.

Even running two paces ahead of me, I could tell she rolled her eyes.

"Hey! Are you coming by today?"

"Probably not," she said. Then she jetted down the path back toward the storage space that was our CrossFit gym, or box as it was called by the other members and the owner, Rob Richards.

Inside, Felicia went straight to her kettlebell and began to swing. I took several gulps of muggy morning air before lifting my own kettlebell between my legs. I took another labored breath and began the set of swings required for the workout.

By the time I got to the pull-ups, Felicia was already at the door starting her next round. There was no catching up with her this time.

But she did come by for coffee.

"This has to be quick," she said. "I've got to get to work."

"Okay. I get it," I said. And I *did* get it. But still, I wanted answers. I rang up her order. This was a first.

Felicia leaned over the counter and peered longingly at the espresso machine. I, of course, knew what she was getting at, but I wasn't ready to make her mocha. Not yet.

She waited for all of another second. "So this is how you're going to play it?"

"I don't know what you're talking about," I feigned confusion.

"Fine," she said. "I'll disclose something about Barb's case if you start making my drink."

I shook my head, smiling. Then I zeroed out the order. "That's good payment for today. But pretty soon I'm going to have to start charging you for these."

"I thought cops drink free coffee," she said.

"They do." I pointed to the five gallon thermos filled with drip coffee.

"You wouldn't."

"Depends how good the information is." I went to work on her latte, drizzling mocha syrup in the bottom of a to go cup.

"Honestly, Kirby, we're running on empty. There just aren't many leads. And there's not enough probable cause—we can't get a warrant for our persons of interest."

"*Persons*?" I asked. "And those are?"

"You know I can't—"

I poured the milk, but I didn't froth it. Instead, the stainless steel container sat on the counter in front of me.

"Seriously?"

"You don't have to say names."

"All right." She sighed. "No names. Let's say I heard about a disagreement between Barb and one of her friends about a week or so before the murder. And let's say it happened at a nail salon that the person owns. Do you know anything about it?"

"Gail?" I asked.

She shushed me with a finger. "We said no names."

"No. We said you don't have to name names. I know exactly whose nail salon you're talking about."

"But do you know what happened?" Felicia asked.

"Not a clue," I said.

"Yeah, well it's not as if they were fist fighting. Two women raising their voices hardly evokes suspicion. Especially those two women. Not a single person we've talked to has an inkling what it was about. And Gail lawyered up. Your Memaw's old boss. She's not saying anything—as is her right. There. Was that good enough *info* for you?"

"Definitely." I nodded and finished her drink.

"How's your gal pal taking it?" she asked. "I'm sure it's been tough."

I squirmed at the mention of Avett. "I don't really know," I said. "I've been giving her space."

"Kirby, are you serious? You need to man up and talk to your girlfriend."

"I will," I said. It wasn't a lie.

"What did you do last night after the funeral?"

"I came back here. I finished the book."

"The book?" Felicia asked.

"You know. *The Dog Woofed Premeditation*. I thought you were as excited about it as me?"

"It took you until last night to finish it?" She laughed. "Sorry, I've moved on since then. I think I finished it Friday night, definitely by Saturday because that's when I took it back to the library."

"And?"

"And I thought it was okay." Felicia shrugged. "Nothing to write home about. I guess I'm not as into her stuff now as I was a few years back. It all seems so contrived. I hate it when the police miss little things—stuff we'd never actually miss."

"Like Ryan's car being towed?" I asked.

"That was different," she countered. "It's not my fault Ross wanted to trust his investigation to some unis. And this book, it was a way bigger mistake. They didn't get photos from the wedding photographer. That's just silly."

I smiled. She was right. I still wasn't sure what had thrown me—why I thought the book was missing something. Maybe she had an idea. I tried bating her. "You didn't think anything else was off?"

"Are we still talking about the book?" she asked.

"Yes."

"Oh, well, I'm never forgiving her for what happened with Cleatus. You don't have to remind me that dogs live an unfairly short life. I mean, seriously, why do that? It's fiction. Let's just pretend he lives until he's forty. Fifty even."

"Agreed." I absentmindedly glanced at Gambit. He perked up, stretched, then sauntered to Felicia for some ear scratching. "But Cleatus *is* actually what bothered me the most."

"His death?"

"No." I pressed the lid down on her coffee. "I don't know what it is. But I think it's got *something* to do with Cleatus."

That afternoon, Sarah and our new hire took over for the day. A guy in his early twenties, Neil used to work at the Starbucks at the outlet mall forty-five minutes away. He'd also briefly driven for the HytchHiker app—which was how I'd first met him.

I had about an hour or so before I was supposed to meet Avett for some house hunting. Even though Holly had returned to New Orleans, their relationship had become strained almost overnight.

I stopped in at the library, deposited *The Dog Woofed Premeditation*, and exited the building. Halfway out, I stopped and doubled back.

My personal collection of books had dwindled over the years. Between moves for the Air Force and leaving a bookshelf's worth at home that my parents boxed up and put in their storage unit, I only had a small row of books on the entertainment center in my studio apartment. None of which were *The Dog Woofed*.

If I wanted to know why something in the last book felt off, this was the best place to figure it out. I found the mystery section and perused to the letter I. The shelf was basically bare. Not even Felicia's copy had made its way back onto the shelf.

A blonde woman probably around my age, was running the information desk. She looked the part of librarian, down to the pair of glasses on a chain around her neck.

"Can I help you?" she asked.

"I think so," I said. "*The Dog Woofed*—I was looking for other books in the series."

"Didn't you *just* return the last one?" She eyed me speculatively. "You know, usually you're supposed to read them in order."

I smiled. "I've read them before. I'd like to get reacquainted."

She nodded. "I understand. You must be Kirby, Felicia's friend."

"I am," I replied. "And you are?"

"Sabrina," she said. Then she tapped away at the keyboard of a computer to the side of her before making a *tsking* sound. "Yes, it looks like they're all out. And even then, most are on hold. We had a run on them after Ms. Isley's book club appearance. You were there, weren't you?"

"I was."

"Me, too," she said, smiling. "Lovely speaker. She comes in here from time to time. I always get a little starstruck."

She tapped the keyboard a few more times.

"Kirby," her tone changed. "I'll put your name on a hold for a few of these. Which books did you have in mind?"

"I don't know. The first couple—the first three," I said.

"Done. You'll get an email when they're available."

"Wait. You have my email?" I asked.

"Felicia," she reminded me with a wink.

14

A day, and then a week passed. Then another. It got easier. We talked about Barb's murder less. Felicia never said anything unless I asked, and I got out of the habit of asking. Life got back to a sort of normalcy. A new normalcy. One with Avett as a constant.

On Fridays, I still met with my gaming crew. But Saturday night was date night. And Sundays were also spent with Avett. We liked to go to the outlets to catch a matinee.

The for sale sign was still there in Barb's yard. There had been a few showings, but no one had made an offer. And Avett wasn't happy with any houses she'd seen. She started looking at rentals and small properties over on Gaiman Island.

We were eating dinner with Memaw on a Tuesday when Avett brought Barb's murder up. It seemed like she was as keen to solve the mystery as I was. Or she was at least open for the discussion.

"I just can't believe they haven't found anyone," she said. "It's been two weeks. You know there's this show that says if they don't find the culprit within forty-eight hours, then they often don't find them."

"I've watched that show," Memaw said. "Kirby, isn't your friend able to tell you anything?"

"You wouldn't like what she's told me."

"Oh? Why not?"

"Because it's about your friend, Gail..."

"Kirby Jackson," Memaw said with venom. "You've known Gail Crabtree your whole life. What makes you think she'd be capable of such a... such a... such a horrible thing."

"Memaw, I'm not saying she did it. I'm just saying there's a *chance* that—okay, yeah, I guess I can see how it sounds like I—"

"Kirby!"

"Calm down." I'd hardly ever seen Memaw get so worked up. She either really didn't think Gail would do such a thing or, more likely, she thought Gail *could* be responsible. And she was trying to talk herself out of it by being angry with me.

"No one's going to jail yet," Avett put in. "But seriously, Kirby, what did Felicia say about Gail?"

"She said they had a fight. They don't know what over."

"And how long have you known about it?" Avett asked. It was her turn for her face to get red.

"A while," I said.

"A while," she repeated.

"There's nothing we can do," I said. "Unless you want to go beat down her door and question her."

"Maybe I do," Avett said.

Memaw did cool down a bit. Avett, too. But the conversation wasn't over. Memaw fiddled with the medical ID bracelet she'd worn since Pawpaw's death.

"It wasn't Gail," she said. "I don't care what you think. She and Barb may've had their differences. But they were on good terms last I checked... At least, I *think* they were. Before that little spat at the nail salon, they hadn't said an ill word about the other for a week, maybe two."

"A record," Avett said, laughing.

I gave her a look.

"What? Kirby, I'd rather laugh than cry." Avett wiped a stray tear from her eye. She wasn't doing well at either. "You know how bad a gossip Aunt Barb was. And you didn't live with her. I think Memaw's right. She hadn't even mentioned Gail lately."

"But they had a fight at Gail's nail salon."

"You know I hate to let other people touch my feet," Memaw said by way of explanation why she wasn't there.

"Okay. We're back at square one," I said.

"No." Avett shook her head. "We *should* at least talk to Gail. I mean if Memaw thinks that's okay. And we won't beat down her door."

It was a question, and it wasn't.

Memaw answered correctly regardless. "Fine, fine. I'm guessing you want me to set it up?"

"You guessed right."

It only took her a couple of days to figure something out. She tried to explain it to us over an impromptu dinner at The Fish Camp.

"So, it's like Painting with a Twist?" Avett asked.

Memaw didn't get the reference. "What is Painting with a Twist?" she asked.

"It's a painting party. Usually the host picks out what everyone is painting. Everyone paints the same thing."

"Right." Memaw nodded. "But what's the twist?"

Avett bobbed her head in contemplation. She didn't

know Memaw that well. "Usually," she said, "it's BYOB, bring your own beverage, booze, or what not."

"There won't be any of that," Memaw informed us. "This is at the Baptist church. And you know about Baptists."

Memaw gave me a knowing wink.

I nodded, smiling at the thought of one of Pawpaw's old jokes.

"What are y'all talking about?" Avett quizzed us. "You know, I'm Baptist."

"Sorry," I told her. "My Pawpaw had a joke. It went something like this: Why do you take two Baptists fishing?"

Avett scrunched her eyebrows. "I don't know. Why?"

"If you take one, he'll drink all your beer."

Avett laughed with us. Memaw laughed the loudest. But I did see a tear roll down her cheek.

"All right. It's settled," I said. "Date night and we're going to an elderly painting party."

"At the Baptist church," Avett said, smiling.

"To discuss a murder," Memaw reminded us. "And don't you two forget, I told you Gail had nothing to do with this."

The fellowship hall at Emmanuel Baptist Church of Niil-haasi was spacious. Circular tables dotted the room like love bugs on a windshield. The lighting was dim, especially considering that we were about to use the space as an art studio. Doubly so after realizing that out of everyone here, Avett and myself were the only two without eyeglasses.

A cluster of senior citizens sat to one side of the room next to a makeshift stage. The instructor was getting set up. She was younger than her elderly students—but not by much.

She gave a wave to me as we approached.

"Mrs. Kyle?" I said, putting the face with a name. Hers was a face I hadn't seen in over fifteen years.

"Kirby." She brought me in for a hug. Mrs. Kyle was my art teacher, not in high school, but in middle school. She'd always encouraged me back then, but she did that for everyone—no matter their level of talent. "It's so good to see you. Your grandmother told me you were coming. And who's this?"

"Oh. Right. Mrs. Kyle, this is my girlfriend, Avett." I stumbled over the words. "Avett this is Mrs. Kyle."

"That's me. His *girlfriend*, Avett." She shook Mrs. Kyle's hand but gave me a mischievous smile. We hadn't really discussed the formality or conventionality of our relationship. We were dating—exclusively dating. In my mind that meant for all intents and purposes she was my girlfriend. This was just the first time I'd said it out loud with her around.

"You can call me Celina. You too, Kirby."

"It's nice to meet you, Celina," Avett said. "We'll go find a seat. I can't wait. I haven't painted in years."

"How about you, Kirby?" Mrs. Kyle asked. "When's the last time you held a paint brush?"

"Ninth grade art class," I answered.

She shook her head, tsking. "What a shame. You had —*have*—talent."

"We'll see."

Mrs. Kyle put her chair between two canvases. One was finished, hydrangeas in two mason jars on a table. The other was a white canvas with a thin penciled outline.

Each table had a few copies of the starting canvas. Beside them were aprons and paints at the ready. We found Memaw at a table toward the back.

"What was all that about?" Avett elbowed me in the ribs.

"All what about? Calling you my girlfriend?"

"No, silly. With Celina. Up there."

I shrugged. "Nothing really. She taught me in middle school—back when Ryan and I were the best of buds. Back then I was going to be a comic book artist. Ryan was going to write them. Dude could barely draw a stick figure. We had a plan."

"And what happened to the plan?"

"Life," I said flatly. She gave me a *look*, forcing me into an answer. "If I tell you, do you promise not to read anything into it?"

"Obviously I can't make that promise. Especially now."

"Then obviously I can't tell you," I said.

"No, Kirby. All right. I promise. What is this *life* you speak of? What came between you two?"

"Felicia started hanging out with us in high school. And by *us*, I mostly mean me."

"So you're saying girls happened. You no longer wanted to be a nerdy little boy drawing superheroes in your basement. I get it. I do. How did Ryan take that?"

I shrugged. "Ryan was Ryan. He found a new hobby— several really. Dungeons and Dragons. He learned to play bass. Not that his comic book dream ever truly died. The shop is one reminder of that. He was actually trying to get me to draw again, ever since I came back."

"And you didn't?"

"No. I was busy managing a failing coffee shop."

"A comic book and coffee shop," she reminded me, pointing the end of her paintbrush at me.

More senior citizens filtered inside while Avett and I chitchatted with Memaw.

Finally, Gail sauntered into the room. But perhaps her

gait was only slow because of her companion. Gail had her hands wrapped around a frail, elderly arm. It was hard to tell which one was leading the other. The old gentleman, I recognized as Dr. Summers, took feeble small steps. Most of his weight rested on Gail—though there wasn't much of it. And he still looked about to fall over.

Dr. Summers had been my dentist when I was younger. Now his practice was in the hands of his grown-up granddaughter. Memaw had attempted to set me up with her twice now, but the idea of dating someone who'd seen the inside of my mouth was off-putting. That and the next closest dentist, should we break up, was forty-five minutes away. I had to politely fend off Memaw's endeavors.

Gail and Dr. Summers took the table beside ours. A few minutes later, things got started. An hour passed. Our paintings were beginning to take shape. I couldn't say mine looked any better than Avett's or vice versa, but both of them were turning out better than Memaw's.

If our paintings were Vincent van Gogh's *The Starry Night*, hers looked more like a Jackson Pollock. The problem —ours weren't *The Starry Night*. Memaw had runny splotches, none of which looked like a *happy accident*. Her jars were misshapen, and her flowers' stems didn't exactly go inside those jars.

"Stop your laughing now, Kirby Jackson," Memaw scolded me. "I'm doing the best I can. I told you this wasn't my forte. And wasn't there a reason we came here? Or are *you* forgetting?"

"I thought *you* said there was no way Gail did it," I whispered.

Memaw scowled. "That was before Gail showed up with Dr. Summers. You know that's who Barb was seeing before she died."

I turned to Avett accusingly. Wasn't that something her roommate should know about? Something she could've mentioned?

Avett shook her head. "They went out to dinner on occasion. I'd hardly call that dating."

"That is exactly what you call dating when you're widowed," Memaw retorted.

Both of them needed to keep their voices down. We were drawing looks from folks around us—including Gail Crabtree.

15

Okay, our reconnaissance hadn't gone that well. But we did come back with a few things, mostly in the form of three paintings. Two decent ones and Memaw's. Well, that, and we thought we figured out what Barb and Gail's rift was over—a man, Dr. Summers. Since jealousy is likely the number one murder motivation on the list of murder motivations, I wasn't going to rule out Gail. Even Memaw was feeling uneasy now.

I texted Felicia that tidbit of information, but she didn't respond. She would hate that I was doing my own quasi investigation. I expected her to tell me as much the following morning.

The back office of Kapow Koffee was probably the best place I had to hang the painting. It wouldn't exactly fit with the shop's motif, not being a portrait of Wolverine, Wonder Woman, or Iron Man. And I didn't keep decorations in the flat upstairs. In my mind, the apartment was a means to an end. One day, I'd move out. Just like Avett was about to do.

Holly and Avett were back on speaking terms. Barb's house hadn't sold, but Avett agreed to move out and help clean out all of Barb's things. She found a condo. It was small but in a gorgeous spot across the bay. And speaking of jealousy... I was only a tiny bit jealous.

After ensuring everything was in order at the store for the next day, Gambit and I retreated upstairs to my own small space. I kept the apartment *reasonably* clean, especially considering the amount of time I spent inside it. It was mostly a space to watch television, read books, and sleep.

Tonight, only two of those things were on my mind. My hold on the first three of *The Dog Woofed* series had been filled. But I'd put off reading them. I'd gotten an email the first book was due next week. Someone else had placed a hold on it. So I had to stop dragging my feet.

It had been about fifteen years since I'd read it the first time. Unfortunately, the book wasn't a fine wine. It hadn't aged well.

But finish it, I did. I was still having trouble finding that certain something that had bothered me about the last book. Putting two and two together was not making four.

I absentmindedly flipped through the pages of the last book again. My finger landed on a passage toward the end and I read on from there.

A line caught my eyes. I read and re-read that same line over and over. Then the lightbulb went off. I went back to the first book and found the exact line I needed there. Then I scoured the third for a similar passage. And found it.

In theory, this was enough to prove my case, at least to myself. Well, that and I only had the three books.

I felt smug the next morning, but I didn't say a word to Felicia at CrossFit. Instead, I waited for her to arrive for her usual morning mocha.

"I figured it out," I told her when she walked inside.

"The murder?" she asked. "Did Gail do it?"

"No, not the murder. Did *you* figure out the murder?"

"No," she said. "And Gail didn't do it by the way. I hope I didn't put you through too much trouble."

"How do you know Gail didn't do it?"

"Forensics," she said. "It rhymes with P-N-A."

"You found DNA? And you haven't caught anyone?"

"Well, the judge won't let me swab everyone from the book reading. Trust me, I asked. And Gail volunteered hers, by the way. That's that."

I nodded. Memaw would be pleased. And there would be a significant amount of "I told you so-ing," in my future.

"What did you figure out then?" Felicia asked.

"The problem with *The Dog Woofed Premeditation*..."

"And what's that?"

"Do you remember the other ten books?" I asked her. "The way the last clue is *always* put together?"

"Remind me," she said. "And are you going to make my drink?"

"Listening to me is your payment today."

"I have five dollars. I'm happy to—"

"Just listen," I said. "There's always a brief scene from Cleatus's point of view—I'm going to check the other books when I return these three to the library. I mean, if there's any available. But from what I remember, it doesn't fail. There's always *always* always one scene where the point of view shifts to Cleatus. It happens so fast you can hardly catch it. But it's there."

"That does a ring a bell," she replied. "And you're sure the last story didn't have it?"

"Not positive," I said. "I've got to check that too. But I'm like ninety-nine percent sure it didn't have it."

"Weird." She bit her lip, eyeing the espresso machine.

"Weird? That's it? You really don't think the book was odd?"

"It's a book," she said. "I read one or two a week. And I'm sorry, but I haven't written a book report since college. What's the big deal?"

"Nothing. I just think it's odd. It didn't *feel* like the other books. It felt forced."

"Maybe it was. You could ask Pam. She's still in town, ya know."

"I know," I said. "Her assistant comes by pretty regularly."

That seemed to jog something in Felicia's mind. "Be careful with her. All right?"

"Why? Is she a suspect?"

Felicia looked away. So, yes.

"Okay," she said. "We know about Barb's connection with Pam Isley. It's pretty cut and dried. They were friends in college, but they fell out—as people do. Do you know much about Doreen? Pam's wife?"

"Only what Wikipedia says," I told her.

"Well, that's more info than I had a few weeks back."

I sighed, shaking my head. But I did start her mocha. "Okay, what about Doreen?" I asked.

"It's not Doreen that matters," she said. "It's the assistant, Kelly Sue. She has a connection to Doreen."

"Okay," I said slowly.

"Here's the kicker. Doreen and her family were estranged. They didn't like the way she lived her life and all that nonsense. You know how it is. Add to that, something else odd. About a year ago, Kelly Sue was paid a large sum from Pam's account. Now, we tracked it down. The claim is it was for ghostwriting. But we're thinking it could be some sort of payoff."

"Why?" I asked.

"That's what we don't know. We thought it could be that Kelly Sue is blackmailing Pam. But Pam vehemently denies that."

"What does Kelly Sue say?"

"We haven't talked to her," Felicia admitted.

I crunched together the timeline that Felicia had laid out. "What if Kelly Sue *did* write that book, *Death of the Family*? She's been in here writing. She has a thriller of her own coming out next year."

"Even if she wrote it. It doesn't mean it wasn't a payoff."

"Right. I get that," I said.

"And think about this." Felicia waited for me to pass her the drink before she finished her theory. "What if Barb ate something *she* wasn't meant to eat. What if it was meant for Pam?"

"If you think she's blackmailing Pam, then why would she try to kill her? Or Barb?"

"You said it yourself. She has a book coming out next year. Maybe she doesn't need Pam anymore."

16

The Niilhaasi library wasn't too far away from the shop, but it wasn't walking distance. The older building that housed it had once been the city hall. A new city hall was built in the late 1980s, and the library was moved here. Like a good book with a bad cover, the library's facade was drab, but its contents made up for it. There were rooms for club meetings, a large space for story time with toys and a small jungle gym, a separate computer room, and the main library was spacious. And it was filled with books.

I returned the books, then went straight to the mystery section. I wanted to confirm my theory. I found two more on the shelf: Book 5, *The Dog Woofed Assassination*, and book 7, *The Dog Woofed Strangulation*. It took all of ten minutes. There it was. In every book, aside from the last, Cleatus had a point of view scene of his own. And his death, at the end of the book, didn't prevent Pam from writing one. He had already helped to solve the case. No, she'd decided to nix that scene for some other reason.

But why? Did she get a new editor? *No.* I checked the

acknowledgments section at the end of the book. Then what was her rationale?

When I went to return the books to the shelf, Sabrina, the librarian, caught me in the middle of an aisle.

"Kirby," she said softly. "It's so good to see you." She took one look at the books in my hands. "Are you still catching up on old reads?"

"Sort of." I tried to mimic her quiet voice, but she had years of practice on me.

Sabrina glanced around, as if checking no one was within earshot. "I finally did it," she whispered. "I talked to her. To Pam Isley. Did you know our very own Barb Simone was the basis for Clementine in her books?"

"I did," I answered. "I'm actually dating Barb's niece, Avett."

"Oh, that's right. I *did* hear that." Sabrina nodded her head mournfully. "You know I hope they find who did it. I've even been asking Felicia about it."

"She's never one to discuss police business," I whispered back. I'd normally feel bad, talking behind Felicia's back like this. But I was pretty sure I knew exactly how Sabrina had found out I was dating Avett.

I was also thinking it's not so hard to get information from Felicia. *All you have to do is bribe her with mochas.* From her intel, I knew that Pam's assistant *could be* linked with Barb's murder. I kept both of those thoughts to myself.

"She isn't, is she," Sabrina agreed. "But that's not what I wanted to tell you. As I was saying, I finally talked to Pam. And when she told me about Barb, well, I had an idea—an epiphany if you will. Have you looked inside our History of Niilhaasi room?"

I shook my head no. There were quite a few rooms in the

library I hadn't ventured inside. I *had*, however, seen signs pointing in its direction.

"There's not too much in there these days." Sabrina realized her voice had gotten louder and lowered it. "There's a history of the library. A history of the town as a fishing village. You know the government owned most of Gaiman Island until well after World War II? There's quite some history there. Old things of Steven Gaiman's. You know he leased the land on a hundred year lease from the government. Then he made way for all of the development of the island."

That much I did know. It was taught in the local elementary school.

"Well," Sabrina clasped her hands together, "I was thinking of making a space for Barb and Pam Isley in the room. A sort of Niilhaasi in literature. Pam says she has some old photos. And that she can bring in some signed books, older editions, and things like that. But I'm wondering, do you think Avett would have anything to contribute?"

"Maybe." I shrugged. "We're actually supposed to clean out Barb's house this weekend."

"Perfect! Well, if you find something, could you let me know? I'd love to get things set up in the next couple of weeks. Pam says she's going back to Vermont for the Christmas holidays. I'd like it set up before then."

That didn't leave a whole lot of time.

"Sure," I said.

"Here. I'll take these back for you." She grabbed the books. "And thank you," she whispered.

She walked away, leaving me there to contemplate, not only the issue with the last book—but what was the situation between Kelly Sue and Pam? Had something between them contributed to Barb's death?

I didn't have to wait very long to find out more.

"Me again." Kelly Sue nudged up against the counter. Behind her was an onslaught—the high school rush. Seven, maybe eight, teenagers crowded behind her, most with their heads down, eyes glazed over, and a phone about three inches from their noses.

Why'd she have to pick now to come in?

I'd been hoping she would come since my talk with Felicia. And I'd asked Neil if she came in while I was on my break.

But with the high schoolers crowding her, questioning would prove to be difficult. If it were my regulars, I could have Neil prepping each and every order. Teenagers proved more difficult. Not only were they hard to distinguish—they seriously all looked the same—but they changed their order daily like they were still trying to find the right coffee to suit their tastes. Like it mattered. Whatever they chose, it was always packed with sugar.

"Americano, right?" I asked her. I readied to pass the order down to Neil, labeling the white mug with a dry-erase marker.

"No, not today," Kelly Sue said. "I don't do coffee after noon. I think maybe a chai tea latte."

Who does she think she is—a high school kid? I rubbed marker off with my thumb and relabeled. I decided not to mention the not-so-insignificant amount of caffeine in a chai tea latte.

"Got it," I said. "You can go ahead and get situated. I'll bring it out to you."

She looked back at the crowd, biting her lip. "Really?"

"Yeah." I nodded. "It's no problem."

I had to find some way to talk to her about these suspicions—and that's all they were, suspicions. *For now.* It was Felicia's job to link her to Barb's death.

Somehow, the stars aligned. Either that or the parents forgot to give these kids their full allowance. Five out of the eight of them, there were eight, ordered drip coffee. Neil handled the two lattes and a frap.

I made Kelly Sue her drink. Then I carefully carried out the chai tea and set it down a good distance from her laptop. She smiled up at me. Her finger was furiously tapping on the down arrow key.

"Are you busy?" I asked her. "Or do you have a minute?"

"For the guy who made my drink and brought it to me, I have a few minutes." She closed her laptop.

I scooted into the opposite side of the booth.

"This will probably sound crazy," I said. "In fact, I'm not sure where to start."

"I find the beginning to be the best place," Kelly Sue said.

"That's right. But you're the writer. It's hard to know where exactly the beginning is."

She took a sip of tea while I focused.

"You've worked for Pam five years. Isn't that what you said?"

"Almost six."

"So you knew Doreen."

She choked on her drink. This wasn't where she must've thought I was going.

"Yes. I knew her. I'd like to say I knew her quite well." She looked down at the table. Either she was a really bad liar, or she was introverted to the point that five minute conversations were taxing. Possibly both. "But I'm not sure what you could say about Doreen that I would deem crazy."

At first, I didn't even know where I was going with this. How was this conversation going to lead to Kelly Sue admitting she tried to poison Pam?

I cleared my throat. And it was like the puzzle pieces had aligned. "I think *she,* that is Doreen, wrote *The Dog Woofed* series. Not Pam."

A hint of a smile flickered across her face before Kelly Sue met my eyes again. It happened so fast I wasn't sure it happened at all. "I don't know what you're talking about," she told me.

"You're not going to deny it?" I asked.

"If I denied it," she said, "you'd just think I was lying. This is one of those Catch-22 scenarios where nothing I can say is right. And saying too much would put me out of a job."

"Well, that sucks." I didn't mince words. "It's not like I'm going to the papers with this. I just wanted the inside scoop on one of my favorite authors."

"Yeah. Well, I'm sorry I couldn't be any more help. Seriously, is Pam *really* one of your favorite authors? You've never heard of Dickens? Fitzgerald? Heck, J. K. Rowling?"

"Maybe I've heard of that last one," I said jokingly.

She put her fingers to her laptop and opened it an inch. A clear indication I was no longer welcome at the booth. But even if she wasn't going to confirm my theory, I still wanted to know more about Doreen. Not everything about her could be part of that nondisclosure agreement.

"One last question. Did you write *Death of the Family*?"

"What do you think?" She grinned.

"I think you got paid for writing it—"

The words had just fallen out of my mouth. Word vomit. I'd been prone to it since I was a kid.

Kelly Sue's mouth fell open.

"How do you know that?"

Think of a lie. Think of a lie.

"Seriously, how do you know that?"

I couldn't think of a lie. "The police did a background investigation on you. Part of the investigation into Barb's murder..."

"Barb's murder?" she asked.

"Yeah."

Her face twitched. "I've got to go," she said.

Then Kelly Sue slammed the laptop closed and she stormed out of the shop.

She might be mad, but that didn't hold a candle to how Felicia would take this. She was going to be furious.

17

That Friday was the homecoming parade. The tigers were on a winning streak. The whole town showed up to support them. The shop was booming.

I hadn't seen a glimpse of Kelly Sue for the rest of the week. And I'd hardly seen Felicia either. After I told her about my confrontation with Kelly Sue, she was less than pleased. She'd even offered to pay for her mocha from now on, and she assured me she would never pay in information again.

With all of the afternoon's business, I'd barely had a chance to let Gambit out to do *his* business. When Sarah got back from throwing candy, she immediately joined me behind the counter and began making drinks. Neil came in an hour later.

I excused myself from the counter. "Gambit needs to go out. We'll be right back," I told them.

With all the commotion still going on in front of the store, I opted to go out back. That was my first mistake. The second was not having a tighter grip on his leash.

He darted out after that same cat. Of all places, it had been atop the dumpster. A perch that a dog less than a foot tall could never reach. Nevertheless, it decided its best move was to make a run for it. Gambit took the bait.

I didn't know what Gambit would do if he caught it. He must not have known either because when he did catch up to the cat, he just barreled into it. Then he barked playfully and scampered back toward me, expecting the cat to chase him.

It didn't.

The cat turned tail and ran the other direction. This time I was able to get ahold of Gambit's leash.

"That's twice," I scolded him. "There *won't* be a third time."

I was still grumbling when we got back to the store. The crowd had thinned out with only a few customers left browsing the comic section. I picked up a broom and decided to vent my frustrations by cleaning up.

Neil kept himself busy grinding coffee beans and mixing mocha powder with water to make syrup. Sarah left for the day.

My back was to the door when a couple walked inside.

Neil greeted them from the counter.

"Hi-ya," he said cheerily. "What can I getcha?"

Getcha... Is that even a word?

"We're looking for Kirby," a man's voice said.

Now, normally Gambit didn't react to customers coming in and out of the shop, but he knew this man's voice. He stretched and groaned which caught Dr. Capullo's wife's attention and her eyes lit up.

"No, no," she baby talked, "that's who we came here to see."

"Hey, Dr. Capullo." I pushed a pile of dust and sand out of the way and leaned the broom against the wall.

"Kirby," he said. "You remember I told you about my wife, Meera. Meera, this is Kirby."

Dr. Capullo was dressed casually. Meera was dressed much the same, except she wore a bindi on her forehead. They must've attended the parade.

"Oh my goodness, he's adorable," Meera announced. "And a dapple. You didn't tell me he was a dapple. They're going to make some beautiful puppies."

She kneeled on the floor beside Gambit and went nose to nose, scratching behind his ears and down his back. She was a dog kisser. And Gambit wasn't one to refuse.

"He likes to make friends," I remarked. Then I did a doubletake. "Wait. What was that about puppies?"

"Cindy's in heat," Dr. Capullo said. "Would you mind bringing Gambit by this weekend?"

"I think I could bring him by tomorrow. But Sunday's booked."

"That's perfect." Dr. Capullo found Gambit's ball on the floor. He bounced it and Gambit bounded away.

"Meera, honey, why don't you get us some coffees for the road? I'll take a pumpkin spice latte."

"Sounds good." Meera smiled. She went up to the counter, and I heard her say, "Two pumpkin spice lattes."

I groaned inwardly. When would this fake fall end?

"I love the shop," Dr. Capullo gestured toward the comic side of it. "I used to collect these things. I was big into the Hulk. I guess it was the whole scientist thing, Dr. Bruce Banner. Who's your favorite?"

I didn't want to admit to him that I wasn't exactly into comics—that I just kept this part of the store open in tribute to Ryan. "I guess Spider-Man," I said.

"Good choice. *Also* a scientist." I wondered about the emphasis. Did he know something I didn't?

Gambit had found Meera once again. The two of them were clearly infatuated. She was enamored of his dapple charms.

Neil called out the two lattes and set them on the counter. Dr. Capullo retrieved them. "We'll be in touch," he said. "And if you know anyone looking for a dachshund, let us know. All right?"

"Sure," I said.

Gambit watched longingly as they left. He'd see them again soon enough.

And as far as someone wanting a dachshund was concerned, I knew Avett was on that list.

18

That Sunday, Avett greeted me on the porch of her Aunt Barb's house with her typical broad smile—but without her usual dark red lipstick. Today, her hair was pulled back in a ponytail. She wore short shorts and a faded old t-shirt from a John Mayer tour many years ago.

My own moving attire was similar, a dusty and faded black undershirt with my last Air Force unit's insignia. The pair of khaki shorts I wore had seen better days. There were rips near the knees and a precarious hole or two that showed through to my boxer briefs. I would've probably thrown them out had they not fit so comfortably.

"I promise," Avett said, still grinning, "it's not *a lot* of stuff. We just need to get my stuff out, then sort through the rest of hers. Richards Heavy Lifting has a service to take things in bulk to Goodwill."

"Right," I said. "Sorting sounds good."

I'd luckily, or maybe unluckily, been away when my parents had done this before moving to Costa Rica. Now most of their things sat in storage—along with the stuff I'd mistakenly left in my old room. I'd only ventured inside that cramped, box-filled unit once—once was enough to know that I'd probably never find my lost, but not forgotten, possessions.

"Okay," Avett motioned to the truck parked in the driveway. "We'll put my stuff in the U-Haul first. For now, trash goes in the garage. And donations will go in the truck's second trip. What's left will be for the estate sale. And what doesn't sell will eventually get moved to the garage. Sound good? Make sense?"

"It sounds like a plan," I said. "I'm guessing your cousin already went through and got the things she wanted to keep?"

"She did." Avett nodded. "It wasn't much. Not that I really blame her. She said I could have anything I wanted. But this *antiquey* old stuff isn't for me either."

"If there's a spoon collection," I told her with a smile, "I might have to take it."

"There might be," she said with a grin. "But you'll have to wait for the sale."

She gave me a peck on the lips when I reached the porch.

Inside, I cleared a path between her room and the front door, moving a stray chest of drawers and a small table out of the way. Then we began emptying the room of the furniture and the boxes she'd packed earlier. Avett's room was the easy part. We packed it up in less than an hour, then dropped everything off at her new condo. Climbing all the way up to the third floor of her condo with her queen mattress set was an adventure.

We returned to the ground level in the cramped elevator. Only a few more trips stood between us and going back to Barb's to sort.

But when the elevator doors opened, we were both taken aback. Pam Isley stood waiting to get in.

"Hello," she said and let us slide past. There was hardly any recognition in her face. *Did she not remember meeting us?*

The doors were closed by the time either Avett or myself processed what had just happened.

"I guess Pam lives here too," Avett said.

"But that was odd, wasn't it?"

"What was odd?"

"That hello," I said. "It was like she didn't recognize us."

"She might not," Avett said. "Or she might have other things on her mind."

"Like Kelly Sue blackmailing her," I offered.

"Exactly like that." I had told Avett all about the confrontation with Kelly Sue at the shop. Unlike Felicia, she and Memaw were on my side. Pam might be in trouble. She just wasn't willing to allow the police to help.

"Do you think we should do something?" I asked.

"I don't know." Avett pursed her lips. "Do *you* think we should do something?"

"Not without backup," I said.

"Backup?"

Memaw knocked gingerly on the door. Pam's penthouse suite was on the top floor, eight stories higher than Avett's condo. We had to take the stairs the last floor up. The elevator wouldn't allow us any higher.

Of the three of us, Memaw was the most worried.

Avett had her own trepidations. "I'm probably breaking some tenant code being up here," she said. "And are you sure this isn't dangerous? What if Kelly Sue is armed?"

I shook my head no. Not that her being armed hadn't occurred to me. But we'd gotten this far. It wasn't time to chicken out now.

"We just need to talk to Pam alone," I said. "If she's being threatened, I have Felicia on speed dial. She can be here in minutes."

Avett gave me a look. One that asked, *Why do you have Felicia on speed dial?*

"You know what I mean," I said, flustered. "I have her number. It's not like she's my first contact on favorites."

"And who's that?" Avett asked coyly.

"Obviously Memaw."

Memaw chuckled. "Hush, you two. Someone's coming."

"Kelly Sue," we heard Pam's voice call out. "Kelly Sue," she called again. Then Pam opened the door a crack. "Can I help you?"

"Pam, hi. It's us," Avett said.

"I can see that," Pam retorted. "And what can I do for you?"

"Can we come in?" Memaw asked. "We'd like to speak to you—it's about Barb."

Pam looked wary. Then she nodded and unlatched the chain on the door.

"Sorry for the intrusion," I told her.

"Yes. I'm sure you are." Pam stopped to think a moment. "Why don't we go to the sitting room? Kelly Sue was just making me some sweet tea, would you like some?"

"I'd love some," Memaw said.

"Kelly, could you bring the whole pitcher when you're finished?" Pam called toward the back of the residence. "And glasses. We have guests."

I was surprised by how different the penthouse was from Avett's lower level condo. This was more like a single story home. The sitting room, as Pam had called it, was what I would deem a library. Sure, there were a few places to sit—a large L-shaped couch, an oversized loveseat, and two fancy reading chairs—but the walls of the room were covered with built in shelving.

Each shelf was filled neatly with hardcover books, some on display like those at a bookstore. These books ranged from literary fiction to genre fiction like romance and fantasy. But there was hardly any mystery. And I noted that none of Pam's books were there either.

Besides books and furniture, the room was tidy and spacious. A glass door on the other side of the room opened to a balcony. It looked out toward the bay while the one on the opposite side of the condo would look toward the gulf and the cream-colored sand beach of Gaiman Island.

"Do you mind if we close the door?" Avett asked Pam. "What we'd like to discuss is, uh, private." Avett peered out into the hallway, looking for Kelly Sue.

"No. I don't mind," Pam said. "But Kelly Sue will be back with the tea shortly."

"Will she knock?" Memaw asked. She took a seat on the large sofa.

Pam looked absentmindedly at the door, then nodded. "She should."

Avett closed the door softly.

I sat next to Memaw on the loveseat while Avett and Pam took the reading chairs. Avett scooted forward in her seat, hands on her knees. She sat as closely to Pam as the chair would allow her.

"So, what is this all about?" Pam's voice was hushed but not a whisper.

"We know," Avett said, her voice in that same tone— hoping Kelly Sue wasn't lurking beside the door, listening.

"You know... You know what?" Pam wasn't defensive, but she wasn't letting anything go either.

"We know everything."

"We know Doreen wrote the original books," I put in. "And we know Kelly Sue is blackmailing you."

"How?" This time Pam's voice *was* a whisper. She looked again at the door. A beat of still silence engulfed the room. "How do you know these things?"

"We just know," I said. "We know you paid Kelly Sue off. And I put together that the last book, well, it wasn't the same as the others... That was you, wasn't it?"

"How do you know?"

"It's missing a scene," I said. Avett nodded in agreement.

"In the original books, you—that is, Doreen—always slipped in one scene from Cleatus's point of view. Always. And without fail. They were sneaky scenes, only a few hundred words. But there was always one."

"That doesn't prove anything." Pam said with a laugh.

"I know it doesn't," I said. "And that's part of why the police can't prove Kelly Sue murdered Barb. They need you to tell them about the blackmail."

I gave Memaw a smile. She sat nervously twisting her thumbs together, probably wondering how we'd talked her into coming up here with us.

Pam looked down at the floor, unwilling to meet anyone's eyes. "Let's say you're right. Let's say Doreen did write the books. It doesn't explain how you know about Kelly Sue..."

"We know she wrote *Death of the Family*," I said. "She was paid for it."

Pam smiled thinly. "She didn't even try to mimic Doreen's style or voice. But the publisher didn't say a word. My agent knows the truth—not the whole truth of course.

Not that Kelly Sue threatened to out me to the world as a fake if I didn't pay her. I had to tell him I was working with a ghostwriter for the last book so I could transfer her the money she requested. That's when she got really greedy. She told me I had to help her to get published herself."

Pam sighed as if a weight had been lifted off her shoulders. In a way, I guess one had. "But that doesn't mean that Kelly Sue—"

"She was trying to kill you," Avett blurted out. "The poison that killed Aunt Barb was meant for you."

"If that's so, then why wouldn't she do it here? She's had a thousand opportunities."

"Because she *is* a mystery writer," I told Pam. "Kelly Sue knew it had to be in a public setting. If it's just you and her here, then where does the blame fall?"

Pam nodded. She knew I was right. There was a long beat of ghostly silence. "Listen," Pam said. "I really should see what's keeping her."

"Sure." We agreed.

I, too, felt as if a weight was lifted. But something caught me.

"Oh, but Pam." I stopped her. "We're not here to confront Kelly Sue. Not yet. My friend, Detective Strong, she says that if you want to press charges she'll be here as soon as possible."

That was a lie. I hadn't talked to Felicia.

"I understand." Pam stood and eased toward the door, still giving us her full attention. "But there's a lot I have to think about. If I do press charges, it's sure to come out that I'm not the writer the world thinks I am."

She opened the door, went into the hall, and closed it behind her.

A few moments later, we heard the clatter of cups. I

stood, but Memaw tugged at my arm. Avett bit her lip uncertainly.

"Kelly Sue... Kelly Sue... Wait!" Pam's voice was loud and panicky. The front door of the condo slammed shut.

Pam rushed back into the sitting room, her eyes red and wet with tears. "She must've been listening." Pam couldn't get a hold of herself. She dropped a piece of paper from her hand.

"What's this?" Avett asked.

"Kelly Sue... she... she tried to leave me this," Pam said. "I caught her before she was finished writing it. Then you heard it. She stormed out."

"What does it say?" Memaw asked.

"It says that she quits," Pam cried. "And that our deal is finished."

Avett scooped the paper off the floor, and she shook her head reading it to herself. "As if blackmail is a deal. Can you believe her?"

"Pam, I have to ask," I said. "Why *did* you let her blackmail you? Surely you know that this day and age, a court would side with you. You're Doreen's family, her beneficiary. Her family wouldn't have gotten anything if it came out she was the writer of the series."

"You're right. That's true," Pam said. "But it's more complicated than that. My backlist doesn't sell as well these days as it used to. It's all about new books. And if Doreen's family did try something, the money could be tied up in a legal battle for years and years to come. Lawsuits aren't done quickly—or cheaply—these days."

Pam found a box of tissues on one of the bookshelves. She dried her eyes. Then she went back into the hallway and grabbed a tray with three quarters filled pitcher of tea.

"It was only a minor spill," Pam said. "We can still have tea if you like."

This didn't sit right with me. I hadn't thought about it before. But if Kelly Sue *was* listening to our conversation then nothing was off the table. She could've poisoned the tea, planning a swift getaway.

"Kelly Sue made that." It wasn't a question. "I think we should pass. I think *you* should too."

"Nonsense, she would never... No, no. I guess you're right."

"Maybe you should call Felicia now," Avett said to me. "Pam, is that okay with you? If Kelly Sue did blackmail you, then she's capable of murder. The police *should* investigate."

"I guess so." Pam set the tray down. "They'll have to know the reason, won't they? They won't keep it quiet. It'll come out that I'm not the author of my books. My name will be ruined... Still, if that's what it costs to catch Barb's killer, let's do it."

"It won't be ruined," Avett soothed. "If we do this right, we can honor both Doreen and Aunt Barb. We can set the record straight *and* right the wrongs of the past few years. Do you trust us?"

"I hardly know you," Pam protested weakly.

She settled back into the reading chair, closed her eyes, and put her fingers to her temples. "Go ahead. Call your friend. If Kelly Sue was involved in Barb's death, well, then we have to know, now, don't we?"

19

"All right, we're here," Felicia said, her eyes on me. She was as angry as I'd ever seen her—which was saying something. "What do you have for us?"

"The tea," I pointed to the pitcher, "we think it's poisoned."

"You *think* it's poisoned?" Yep. Felicia was frustrated. "What makes you *think* that?"

"Come on. You know why." I'd explained as much over the phone.

Felicia gave me a look that said a whole lot more to me than it may've to everyone else. What it said was that she'd told me about Kelly Sue in confidence and I'd broken that trust not once but twice.

"Tell me, again, what happened?" she asked.

Avett spoke up. "Pam left. She found Kelly Sue writing this note." Avett handed Felicia the note. "They had an argument. And Kelly Sue stormed out."

"She stormed out?" Felicia asked Pam.

Pam nodded. "Yes. She did. She said she quit. But as you can see, this note says it all."

Felicia read it over, then handed it to her partner, Detective Ross.

"It's not much to go on," he told Felicia.

"I know. It's not," she said.

"Kelly Sue. She lives here, right?" Ross asked.

"She does," Pam said. "I can take you to her room if you like. You wouldn't need a warrant for that, would you?"

"Actually, we would," he answered. "Detective Strong?"

He cocked his head toward Felicia who already had her phone out.

But then I interrupted. "What about the blackmail?"

"There is that," Felicia agreed.

"All right." Ross scratched the scruff on his chin. "We're not taking this tea in for testing. But with a warrant, I will go take a peek in her room. And you *are* willing to give us a statement, Ms. Isley? Is that right?"

"I am," Pam confirmed.

"We'll do that while Detective Strong calls for a warrant," Ross said.

The warrant arrived while Pam gave her statement. Detective Ross put on a pair of gloves, and Pam led him down a hallway to what had been Kelly Sue's room. Felicia wouldn't allow us back there to look at it. When he returned he held a small vial of a clear-ish liquid.

"This," he said, "I'm willing to go test."

Pam sighed and gave the three of us a forlorn nod. "I'm sorry this ended in this way. But I'm sure these detectives will sort it all out."

"Are you asking us to leave?" Memaw knew a goodbye when she heard one.

"Yes," Pam said. "I think *they* can handle it from here."

❧

We ate a late lunch at Mo's Hideaway and picked up Gambit before returning to Barb's. He spent the car ride in one of his new favorite laps. Avett stroked his back.

"Pretty soon I'm going to have one of your babies," she told him.

I shook my head. "What are we going to do with a bunch of little Gambits running around the city?"

"You should get one too!" Avett suggested.

"No," I said. "We're fine on our own. Aren't we, boy?"

He didn't acknowledge me.

"Do you think they'll catch her?" Avett asked. "Kelly Sue, I mean."

"I knew who you meant. But I don't know. I guess she's on the run. And Felicia won't answer my texts."

Out of the corner of my eye, I thought I saw Avett make a face.

We spent the better part of the afternoon at Barb's place emptying the cabinets and shelves.

The last room we tackled was the master bedroom. It was unspoken, but it was easily the room that made both of us uncomfortable. This was where Barb had slept each night. This was her private quarters. It felt like we were prying into her inner sanctum.

"Is this where you've been all afternoon?"

Gambit was curled up at the bottom of Barb's closet. He perked up, stretched, and disappeared inside the sea of clothes.

"I think all of these have to go to donation." Avett pulled on the sleeves of a cream blouse. "People don't buy clothes in estate sales, do they?"

"Your guess is as good as mine."

"Hmm. How did I know you were going to say that?"

I shrugged. "It's probably just a sign that my witty banter

is losing ground with you. Next it'll be my ruggedly hand-some good looks."

"I think you mean your boyish charm," she countered. "And there's got to be a few more years left there." She kissed my cheek.

"Thanks!" I rolled my eyes. "Then you want me to take all this to the garage?"

"Yeah—if you don't mind. I think maybe we should separate them: dresses, blouses, skirts, et cetera."

We separated the clothes into piles and I placed each one in a bag meant for Goodwill. The closest was mostly bare save a hundred or so hangers. But a worn cardboard box caught my eye. It had been hidden behind the long dresses in a dark corner of the reach-in closet.

Gambit nudged at it with his nose.

"I scooted that back there after the police did their search," Avett said. "I think it was under her bed. What do you think? Trash or donation?"

"It's a box," I said. "Don't we have to look inside it to see where it goes?" This wasn't the first box we'd come across. I'd emptied Barb's storage closet of her Christmas and other holiday decorations. But this one wasn't labeled like the others had been.

"I don't know," Avett said. "It's weird. It still feels like prying even when we've been emptying drawers all day."

"No, I get it," I agreed.

Gambit nudged the box again. He was clearly in disagreement with us.

"It does feel off," I said. "Opening it in her room like this."

She considered that. "Let's take it to the living room. We're finished in here anyway. Is that good with you, Gambit?"

He huffed approvingly.

Avett was right. The box was heavier than I anticipated, like a box full of books. In fact, I could tell it *was* a box of old books. But the weight was lopsided. It was a box not meant for books. The cardboard was flimsy, the tape on the underside even more so.

It felt as if the contents would spill out long before I reached the living room. Gambit snaking between my legs didn't help. But the box held. I set it down on the rug at the foot of the couch. I had to struggle not to picture Barb there when we found her.

Avett sat down beside me, so close our knees were touching. And Gambit lunged into my lap. I let Avett open the folded flaps.

"It's probably just..."

"Junk," I tried to finish her sentence for her. But she was already digging in the box, her mouth agape.

20

"Can you believe this?" Avett asked. She set a stack of letters next to the one of books already on the coffee table.

"I can." I read the spine of each book, counting them in my head. *The Dog Woofed Murder, The Dog Woofed Poison, The Dog Woofed Death.* Each book was signed, not by Pam, but by Doreen. The letters were written with the same scratched out handwriting and signed with that same signature.

Avett rummaged through the remaining contents of the box. There was an old tennis ball and a collar. On its tag, in barely there letters, it read *Cyrus*.

"I guess this was what Gambit was after." Avett held up the ball. "He must've smelled it." She threw it down the hallway and Gambit bounded after it, tail wagging.

We both took turns reading through the letters, then over each note in the books.

"What do you think this means?" Avett asked.

I shrugged. "I think it means your Aunt Barb knew that Pam was a phony. She knew it before any of us."

"Do you think that means..."

"I don't know what it means," I said honestly. "There was poison in Kelly Sue's room, wasn't there?"

"There was," Avett agreed.

"And the way she acted when she found out she was being investigated—that was squirrelly, wasn't it?"

"It was. You're right. I just feel weird. Like maybe Aunt Barb *was* the target."

"Maybe she was," I said. "If she knew about Doreen, well, maybe she put it all together. Maybe she figured out that Kelly Sue was blackmailing Pam."

"And Kelly Sue couldn't have that, could she?"

"No, she couldn't."

Avett bit her lip. Her lips were way too pretty for that.

"What do you think we should do with this stuff?" she asked. "I feel weird about keeping it."

"I know exactly where it should go," I said.

We agreed to meet Sabrina and Pam on Tuesday afternoon at the library. Felicia wasn't talking to me. And according to the news, there was none. No news. No arrest. No nothing. With the exception of one small tidbit—the story we'd already put together. And it turned out not to be such a bad thing. Pam's sales were skyrocketing. It was like that saying, "Any press is good press."

The cardboard box was just as heavy as I remembered it. We had packed it back up with Barb's memorabilia, the signed books and her correspondence with Doreen. The weight it carried was far more than the thirty or forty pounds in my hands. It carried a lifetime's worth of hiding

—hiding the truth that Doreen was the author of *The Dog Woofed* series, hiding her secret and ongoing relationship with Barb, and hiding Barb's own love for the series that she inspired.

I let the box rest down at my waist as we waited for Pam to get out of her Cadillac. Avett put her hand on my neck and playfully scratched the scalp at the back of my head. "I promise this is the last box you'll have to touch for a long while. The movers have got the rest."

"It's no problem," I told her honestly.

The move had given us ample time to spend together outside of the normal dating routine. Our habits had become predictable—Tuesday nights, dinner with Memaw, Thursday nights at her place, Saturday night dates, and Sunday matinees. It was like we'd become an old married couple in only a couple of months of dating.

I thought I spoke for both of us, in not wanting to become an old married couple not even when I got old and married.

Pam offered us a weak smile. It was hard to tell what she might be feeling. Was she happy that everything had come to light? Or angry? She had to be happy about the book sales.

Of course the way it had all played out, well, that was troubling in its own regard. But Pam looked herself, put together. She carried her handbag with both fists, held tightly at chest level.

"Are you ready for this?" Avett asked her.

"As ready as I'll ever be," Pam said.

She had told Avett that her agent and a representative from her publisher would be flying in from New York later tonight. Her agent was the only other person to know about

Doreen's writing, well, other than Kelly Sue, who'd put it together herself. Like I had.

I assumed Kelly Sue had gotten as far away from Niilhaasi as was possible. That was the only explanation as to why there wasn't any news about her. But usually, when there's a manhunt—or in this case a womanhunt—they at least publicize it.

Why hadn't they?

Sabrina waited for us in the entry hall into the main library. She directed us toward the room labeled History of Niilhaasi. It was right next to the large space used for story time and early voting every two years.

"This is exciting, isn't it," Sabrina said—it wasn't a question. The head librarian was positively beaming. "We've got the news coming tomorrow morning for the exhibit opening. And not just the local crew. Someone from *The Times* and *The Post* are going to do a piece. It's such big news."

"It is." Avett smiled.

"And Pam." Sabrina changed her tone. "I don't want you to think that we're discounting your contributions in any way. We understand that the situation has complexities that no one will ever understand. Your role, even if you only wrote the one book, is still a critical component of the overarching story. You were, and still are, the face of *The Dog Woofed* series. So, please let me know if anything here is troubling to you, and we can remove it."

"Thank you." Pam nodded. "I'll let you know."

"Well," Sabrina clasped her hands together, "I have you all set up in here. There should be more than enough space in this display cabinet to get started. Avett, I figure you could do something more centered on Barb—on her history —over here."

Sabrina led Avett over to a sturdy cabinet beside the wall. A framed picture of Barb and Cyrus were already displayed prominently at the center.

"I love this picture," Avett said.

"Me, too. Pam's been such a good sport." Sabrina continued to beam.

I set the box down at a table in the center of the room.

"Oh, I shouldn't forget." Sabrina pointed to me, remembering something. "I'll go get the other one."

"The other one?"

But Sabrina was out of the room. She came back a few minutes later with a smaller box in her hands.

Pam asked, "Where did *this one* come from?"

Sabrina gave her an odd look. "Oh, you know," she said. "Your assistant brought it by."

"When did she do that?" The words slipped from my mouth.

"About a week ago." The librarian could sense our unease, and Sabrina had no reason to suspect this package was anything other than some additional *Dog Woofed* memorabilia.

"Thanks!" I took the box and set it beside the other. A week ago was when Kelly Sue and I had talked at Kapow Koffee.

"We'll let you know if we need anything else," Avett said, hoping Sabrina would take the hint.

"Please, do." Sabrina did retreat to the main library, but she didn't seem especially happy about it.

"What do you think is in here?" I asked when the librarian was out of earshot.

"I believe I know." Pam took a deep breath. She sat her purse down and rummaged through it, nodding at something. "More correspondence. These are the letters that Doreen kept. These are how Kelly Sue entrapped me in the first place."

"Then why would she—"

Pam put a hand up to stop Avett. "I can't say. I'm not sure what game she was playing. Maybe she thought Sabrina would read them and put things together."

"But that would ruin her blackmail," I said.

"I'd already put a stop to it. I told your friends, the police, as much." Pam took a tissue and wiped her nose. "Well, not me really. But the publisher. They called her last week and said they were no longer interested in publishing her book."

"Oh." I nodded. But something about this wasn't adding up.

"Do you mind if we take a look at these?" Avett asked Pam. But before Pam could answer, her hands were already on the top of the box.

"Not at all," Pam said. "I wouldn't mind taking a peek myself. It's been a long time since I've read them."

Avett took the stack of faded letters from the box and divided them. There were years and years of letters from Barb.

What I found in my stack surprised me. It probably shouldn't have. After all, I knew Barb Simone well enough.

Where Doreen's letters had been thankful for Barb's support and for her honest critique of the work. These letters were *mostly* critique. And *not* the two thumbs up kind.

Barb wasn't a fan of the fantasy—the notion that Cleatus, the dog, could help solve murders in any capacity. She didn't like the way that Clementine spoke—or the way that

Clementine got herself into jams. And she especially didn't like the way Clementine got herself out of said jams.

These reviews were much harsher than I'd anticipated. They told a different story than what we read in Doreen's letters.

I perused several before giving my eyes a break. Avett gave me a funny look. Her eyes went wide, and she frowned. Her stack of letters must've read in the exact same way.

Pam nodded to herself, sifting through them. She skimmed, reading just enough to get the gist. I assumed she'd read them all before and she was now looking to ensure we didn't display something that put Pam, Doreen, or Barb into a bad light.

Avett's phone rang. She looked down at it, then sighed. "It's the real estate agent. He said he might call with news. Someone's finally put in an offer."

She answered. "Darwin, hi. Can you give me one second? Let me get out to where we can talk." She scooped up her unread stack and put them beside mine. Then she hurried out of the library with the phone to her ear.

I examined my own phone. I absentmindedly checked Facebook and realized I was doing more reading. I blackened the screen with a tap of my finger and switched it to silent mode. I thought if we finished here fast enough I could take Avett to dinner.

Like Pam, I started to skim through the letters in Avett's stack. The first two were more of the same. But the next letter stopped me cold. This one wasn't in Barb's neat cursive. Instead, it was in Doreen's familiar scrawl.

Why is a letter from Doreen in this stack?

I began to read.

· · ·

Dear Barbara,

Yes, Barbara. Not Babs. Not Barb. I hope this conveys to you the seriousness of this letter...

This letter. This one, I've rewritten and rewritten more times than any draft of a novel. Still, who knows if I'll actually find the guts to send it this time.

Still reading?

I know I haven't written in a few years. We haven't truly spoken in over a decade. I'm told that's just how some friendships go.

And yet you remain one of my dearest and closest friends. Although I realize now that you might've become something different in my mind—a cross between your college self and the storybook version of you I call Clementine.

To see you in person would only confirm my deepest fears and regrets.

But my regrets aren't the reason I'm writing you. Not really.

You see, Barbara, I'm dying. It's a reality I've come to terms with—to grips with. And I've realized that I have no legacy. No family, save a girl I've only just met.

And when you get to the end of your days, realizing such a tragedy as this, well, it starts to wear on you.

Pam's not going to like this. But I've decided that I want my name to be attached to my books. I want the world to know that it was me who wrote them.

Yes, I know I'm no Harper Lee. The world won't remember me for much. But it's my wish.

I'm writing to you because you're the one person I trust to make it happen. You see, I've told Pam and our agent about it. And there's been lots of floor stomping. Lots of heel dragging. And I just don't know if it's going to happen or not.

I'm lying here in this bed, and this is my only outlet. To write to you—to ask you to do me this favor.

Can you?

Forever your friend,

    D.

21

"I see you found it." Pam's voice was like ice. "Don't say I didn't try to prevent it. But your girlfriend, she just had to read these letters. And you—this whole time—you wouldn't leave well enough alone. It would've stopped at Barb if you just hadn't..."

"Hadn't what?" I asked.

"Kept meddling," she snapped. "You're even worse than Kelly Sue was. I should've known better than to stay here. I would've turned tail and gone back to Vermont if I didn't think the police would find it suspicious."

Pam dug around in her purse. This time, not for tissues. Something metallic glinted in her hand. The reality settled over me—I was in the room with Barb's murderer.

"I should've known better," she repeated.

I could stall her, just long enough for Avett to get back. But then I'd be dooming us both.

I had to do something. My hand still rested on my lap, just beside my silenced phone. I inched my thumb over and pressed on the home button. I hoped my muscle memory would remember how to call Felicia, the second person in my favorites, after Memaw.

"I think I should *call Felicia*," I said. "And let her know there's more evidence."

"Evidence against whom?"

"Kelly Sue," I lied.

"Come now, you know it links me just as much as it does her—if not more so. Don't play dumb. You think it was Kelly Sue who blackmailed me when it was me who blackmailed her."

"How?" My voice was that perfect library volume. A whisper.

"Kelly Sue signed a nondisclosure agreement. She couldn't out me if she wanted to—otherwise her own publishing career would be in ruins. I'd sue her for the damages she caused. I'd be entitled to every advance she ever received."

"But she had this," I said.

"Which meant nothing by itself. I made sure there was no other record of Doreen's handwriting. This could be a forgery. Couldn't it? Up until you two found Barb's box of letters."

"That's why you killed Barb…"

Pam nodded.

"Did you kill Doreen too?"

"Now you get it."

"And what about Kelly Sue—where is she now?"

"That I don't know," Pam said. "She really did write that letter. Just not when you three were there."

We never had seen Kelly Sue that day. It was all a show —a ruse. And the evidence in her room, Pam had planted it there.

Click.

The small sound sent a shudder down my spine. I'd seen enough movies and TV to know exactly what it meant.

"We can play this one of two ways," Pam said. "You can give me that paper, and we can pretend your eyes never saw it. Or—"

"Or what?" I asked boldly.

She trained the gun on me. The thing was so small it barely registered as a threat. It was mostly pink aside from the chrome barrel. It *almost* looked like a toy.

"Or this." Pam gestured with the small gun.

"You'd really shoot me?" I asked. "It's much different from poison. You think you'd get away with that just like you did with Barb? Just like Doreen? There are witnesses."

"There's no witness in this room," Pam pointed out. "There's you and there's me. There's my story—and a story no one will hear."

"And what will your story be?" I was trying to buy time.

"My story is simple. Trust me. That's what living with a mystery author all these years has taught me. The simpler, the better. It also helps to be part true. See, you accused me of being Barb's killer. *Truth.* And you put your hands on me. You attacked me. Are you aware of Florida's stand your ground law? I won't spend a night in prison. They'll be thanking me tomorrow. I can see the headlines, *Deranged Fan Attacks Author.*"

"The thing is," I said. "You aren't the mystery author you think you are. Far from it." Slowly, I put the phone on the table, hoping without hope that it wasn't a bluff—that there was someone listening on the other end of the call. "In fact, you just committed one of the worst crimes in fiction. You admitted everything to a cop."

The phone screen glowed. I tapped to put it on speaker. "Felicia, did you catch everything?"

"I believe I did," Felicia's voice erupted from the phone. "Hold tight, Kirby. Units should be right outside."

everal weeks later, we met in the backyard at Dr. Capullo's house. His very nice house. The yard wasn't much, but it was enough for two grown dachshunds and five tiny dachshund puppies.

Neena and Avett had already picked out their two. Neither had decided on a name yet. Meera was keeping one of the girls and naming it after another princess, Belle. It would be another few weeks before they could bring the puppies home.

I was proud to see Gambit doing his part, shepherding his younglings around the yard. Dr. Capullo offered me a beer, which I accepted with gratitude.

It had been a trying few weeks. Even today, Felicia was barely speaking to me.

"I miss my favorite customer," I told her.

"I thought you said I wasn't a customer."

"I didn't mean it," I said.

"If that's the case, I'll be by tomorrow for the usual."

"Sounds good."

"You're probably wondering what happened to Kelly Sue, aren't you? I can tell."

She was right. I *was* wondering.

Felicia nodded. She watched Neena cuddling with a baby dapple, basically Gambit's mini me.

"Kelly Sue came to us," Felicia said. "She'd already quit working for Pam. And she thought Pam might've been responsible for Barb's death. She didn't know how. We reconstructed the events of the night of book club. Gail had set out her pear salad. And Gail doesn't like cherries, so she put a jar of maraschino cherries to the side. And Kelly Sue, who is from the South and knows about pear salad, put a cherry on Pam's plate."

"I remember," I said.

"We speculate that Pam poisoned the cherry. And she traded her *salad* for Barb's, telling her that she didn't like cherries."

"Clever," I said.

"We needed her DNA to prove anything. That stunt you pulled at her place, I thought it would set us back. But it helped. We found the same DNA on the vial of poison. And it wasn't Kelly Sue's. But we still needed to tie it to Pam. Gail gave us her book from the book signing. It had only two sets. Hers and the one by the signature, proving quite definitively the other DNA was Pam's. The confession over the phone is just gravy."

"I don't like gravy," I said. Which wasn't true at all—what I didn't like was having a gun pointed in my direction.

She smiled. "It looks like you're all right. Maybe next time you'll listen to me and stop snooping around criminal investigations."

"Maybe next time," I repeated.

Felicia shook her head.

Neena came over with her puppy cradled in her arms. "Be careful, sweetie," Felicia said. She scooped the puppy to safety in her own arms. "Seriously, Kirby. You don't want one?"

Avett strolled over, her own puppy pressed softly into her chest. "Yeah, you really don't want one? We could keep the family together."

I sighed. "I told you, I'd rather adopt a rescue."

"Then you should," Meera said. "Here, let's get these guys back to their mommy."

Avett and Felicia followed Meera across the yard.

Dr. Capullo smiled and he whispered to me, "You're never going to hear the end of this until you do find that rescue... Remember what happens when this lot gets an idea in their heads."

This was never the plan, I told myself. *How was it again that I'd been talked into coming here?*

I thought I could easily turn around and walk away. But the thing no one ever tells you—or no one ever told me—is once you're inside a place like the animal shelter it becomes impossible to walk away.

No matter how ugly, homely, big, or small, I'd want to take home every single animal I saw there.

"What type of dog do you have now?" the shelter coordinator, her name was Wanda, asked.

"A dachshund," I said.

"Stubborn, aren't they?" she laughed.

"Yeah. But he's a good one."

"Whatever you say, sweetie." She nodded to herself.

"Hmm. A male dachshund. And what type of place do you have? A lot of room to run? A fence? Or what?"

I hadn't really thought about this question—another indicator that I hadn't thought this through.

"It's a small space," I said. "I have a studio apartment, but the dog would have run of the store, too."

"The store?" she asked.

"The coffee shop on Main. Kapow Koffee. That's my store."

"I've seen that place," she said. "I like your sign."

She led the way into the area where the dogs were kept in small fenced-in cages. Each one opened to the outside via a doggy door. There was howling and barking and a whole other array of doggy sounds.

"Now, sugar, I hate to say it, but I'm not sure we have anything that'll suit you. In fact, we haven't had a dog under thirty pounds in about six months. Of course, that's all up to you. If you're willing to go on long walks and buy separate dog food—the big bag kind—then, honey, you can take your pick."

"Really?" I felt foolish. "No small dogs?"

I had a puppy offered to me a week ago, one that Gambit would always have a connection with, father and son. Why had I let that opportunity go? I thought I was going to rescue a needy pup. Now things didn't look so good.

There wasn't a single dog that didn't catch my eye in some way. Most were mixes, part Labrador or part Bull Terrier. Each dog had eyes begging me to take them home.

"Is it only dogs you're after?" Wanda tilted her head in question. Stupidly, I didn't understand where the question was going—again because I hadn't *really* thought this through.

"What do you mean?" I asked.

"I *mean* is it only dogs you're after? We have a whole mess of cats. A cat would be perfect for a studio apartment. Get yourself a scratching post and a kitty litter box, you're in business."

I scrunched my face, failing to hide how silly I thought this line of questioning was. "But dogs and cats—"

"They learn to live together," she said. "Trust me. I have two cats and two dogs. And in here, we have a couple of cats who are used to dogs."

Without realizing it, I was still following Wanda. And she had led us to a different part of the shelter—the place where fifteen or twenty cats were all confined to one room.

"Here we go. What do you think?" She pointed.

The cats were all doing catty things. Leaping up high on cat trees. Sleeping. Eating. I guess those are the only three things they do.

Then one caught my eye. It was the cat from the dumpster behind the shop. The black one with the white spot on its chest. It had the same green eyes. And it was watching me.

"That one came in the other day," Wanda said. "We're calling her Rogue cause she likes to keep to herself."

Now I knew enough about comic books to be dangerous. I did technically own a comic book shop. And the name rang a bell. My dog's name was Gambit, a comic book superhero from X-Men.

"Rogue," I said.

"Yeah, like being solo."

"Or like the mutant," I said under my breath. "Another one of the X-Men."

It turned out, the decision was never in my hands.

ALSO BY CHRISTINE ZANE THOMAS

Food File Mysteries starring Allie Treadwell

The Salty Taste of Murder

A Choice Cocktail of Death

A Juicy Morsel of Jealousy (Jan 2019)

The Bitter Bite of Betrayal (Feb 2019)

Comics and Coffee Case Files starring Kirby Jackson and Gambit

Book 1: Marvels, Mochas, and Murder

Book 2: Lattes and Lies

ABOUT CHRISTINE ZANE THOMAS

Christine Zane Thomas is the pen name of a husband and wife team. A shared love of mystery and sleuths spurred the creation of their own mysterious writer alter-ego.

While not writing, they can be found in northwest Florida with their two children and schnauzer, Tinker Bell. When not at home, their love of food takes them all around the South. Sometimes they sprinkle in a trip to Disney World. Food and Wine is their favorite season.

This is Christine's fourth book.

ABOUT WILLIAM TYLER DAVIS

After leaving the Shire, William "Tyler" Davis was an exchange student at Hogwarts School of Witchcraft and Wizardry. Sorted into Ravenclaw house, he spent many years there before taking time off to companion the Doctor around space and time. He found his wife Jenn while searching wardrobes for Narnia. They settled down in Florida (of all places) to begin adventures with two halflings that like to call them Mommy and Daddy.

After ten years of half-finished stories, he finally finished something. He stored that one away.

Then he wrote the Epik Fantasy series, a humorous fantasy about a halfling who wants to be a wizard.

A lover of *The Hardy Boys* and *The Cat Who, Comics and Coffee Case Files* is his first cozy mystery series.

ACKNOWLEDGMENTS

This book, even at 35k words, was one of the most difficult to write. There are so many people I'd like to thank for their help through this process.

Jenn, my alpha reader, always helps keeps track of the little things. Ellen, my editor, thanks for keeping track of the big things. My mom, my beta reader, finds the typos when everyone else's eyes glaze over them. And thanks to Jason, my first reader, for trying out a new genre.